SUMMER DANGER

Jim Toner

TABLE OF CONTENTS

About The Author 1
Dedication 2
Acknowledgements 3
Chapter One 5
Chapter Two 14
Chapter Three 26
Chapter Four 36
Chapter Five 49
Chapter Six 65
Chapter Seven 77
Chapter Eight 90
Chapter Nine 104
Chapter Ten 114
Chapter Eleven 124
Chapter Twelve 137
Chapter Thirteen 148
Chapter Fourteen 157
Chapter Fifteen 169
Chapter Sixteen 182
Chapter Seventeen 195

ABOUT THE AUTHOR

Jim Toner has loved mystery novels since he was eight years old. He was an exchange student in Tours, France. He has visited several other areas of France including Royan. His previously published novels are the young adult mysteries *Under the Blood* and *The Purity Ring Murders*. He lives in North Tonawanda, New York with his wife Lisa and their cat Olay.

DEDICATION

For Robert L. Cummings, my German professor, who encouraged me to keep writing and Paul F. Johnson, one of my French professors, who introduced me to the novels of many French authors.

ACKNOWLEDGEMENTS

First and foremost, I want to thank my Lord and Savior Jesus Christ for making the publication of this novel possible. He has given me the ability to write and learn other languages.

A huge thank you to Jonathan K. Miller and Devorah Fox of iFlow Creative, who kept the vision for the novel alive.

I am blessed to be a member of the Writers Church. This group has been a huge source of encouragement.

Thank you to Murder in Ice, a division of Sisters in Crime, especially Lissa Marie Redmond and Kathy Kaminski, who answered my questions about police work.

Thank you to Brandon Deppen, the former chief of police of the City of Warren, Pennsylvania, Captain Jeff Dougherty and Sergeant Scott Taylor of the City of Warren Police. They answered questions as to how a small city police department operates.

To Germaine Turpault, her late husband Claude and her daughter Anne, my host family in Tours, France. I could not have had a better host family.

To Professor Jean-Louis Roederer, one of my French professors at Houghton College who practically taught me French.

To the late Joseph Miranda, my high school language teacher, who encouraged me to continue learning foreign languages.

To the North Tonawanda Writers Group. Some of its members saw earlier versions of this novel. Their feedback was invaluable.

For friends and fans who have encouraged me to stay at the keyboard, such as my best friend Jay Taylor, Jeff Cronus, Keith and Jane Scouten, Pastor Jim Vigil, Darlene Irish and her daughter Kathy among others.

And of course, my biggest thanks to my wife, Lisa, who gave me an ambience of love, even through the rigorous times. Her stability, quiet strength and love of books made this journey easier to travel. (She also has published works, but non-fiction). Thanks, darling, for all you do.

CHAPTER ONE

"I can help you with your luggage," said Gil Leduc as he boarded the bullet train at Gare Montparnasse in Paris, France.

He was relieved to be back in his native country after a four-year absence. Homesick didn't begin to describe what he felt while he was away. No place on earth could compare to France.

The seventeen-year-old followed an elderly lady in a long, light blue coat struggling to place a heavy suitcase on the high rack.

"That would be nice, young man," she replied in a high pitched, frail voice. "Be careful though. Don't want you getting hurt."

He lifted and placed the suitcase on the rack with ease. "Wasn't too heavy."

"Good to have a nice, strong man around."

He gave her a small smile of appreciation and followed her toward his assigned seat. The lady sat in front of him with her Bichon Frisé. The dog reminded him of a living ball of cotton.

"Where are you going, young man?" she asked.

"Royan." He couldn't wait to spend some time on the beach with his cousin Catherine. Although he had not seen her in four years, email and social media allowed them to keep in touch and maintain their bond.

"You are visiting from somewhere else then?"

"Yes. I live in the U.S., in Niagara Falls."

She nodded. "You flew over then? To Paris, and now you're taking the train the rest of the way?"

"Right."

"I'm traveling to Royan as well." The lady in the blue coat smiled. "My name is Valerie Cartier. Perhaps we can have a drink together there."

Gil gave her a polite smile. "We'll see." Although Gil usually didn't mind talking to elderly people, he didn't want to agree to spend time with someone he didn't know.

Madame Cartier drew a picture from her handbag. "Perhaps you could meet my granddaughter. She's beautiful, isn't she?"

Gil studied the photo of a teenaged girl with long, brown hair, soft brown eyes, and an olive complexion.

"Is something wrong, young man?" the woman said after a moment. "You don't think she's beautiful?"

"Not at all. She certainly is. Still, I'll decline, thanks all the same."

Madame Cartier pouted. "I'm concerned because she's never had an actual boyfriend. I'm sure she would be delighted—"

"Please. I'm not interested. I have a girlfriend." Gil settled in his seat. He opened the newspaper he'd picked up at the station and made a show of flapping it open, hoping Madame Cartier would cease pestering him. An ad for "The Lion King" movie, sure to be one of summer 2019's international blockbusters, filled an entire page.

The train left the station on time. Gil leaned back and yawned. During the flight from Toronto, he had slept only three hours. He hoped to sleep some on the way to Niort, where he would change trains. Too tired to focus on the newspaper, he was about to set it aside when the leader for a small item caught his eye: Missing American Student. A foreign student in Royan had disappeared. Her fellow travelers reported that they hadn't seen her as expected. Gil was aware some Americans from his area were studying in Royan and he wondered if this missing Ashley Slick was part of that group. The mystery irked him, as mysteries did.

With an uncle and a grandfather in law enforcement, curiosity seemed to be his legacy. Gil had an idea that he was acquainted with the missing girl but before he could pursue it his weariness overtook him.

He was jarred awake when someone grabbed his arm. A conductor towered over him.

"Bonjour. Billet, s'il vous plait."

Ticket, of course. Gil pulled his ticket out of his notebook and handed it to the conductor, who punched it.

Gil stared out the window. The sunshine excited him despite his weariness. He couldn't wait to hit the beach.

At one o'clock the train stopped at Niort. Gil offered to help Madame Cartier with her luggage again, grateful that she left him alone for the remainder of the trip.

"Thank you, young man. You're so kind. I'll keep an eye on yours. No backpack for you? All the young people use backpacks, it seems."

"No," Gil replied. "Just these." He toted a blue duffle bag and a wheeled suitcase.

Gil studied the old woman's face. She had blue eyes and a small nose. Even more than her granddaughter in the photo, she struck Gil as familiar. "Have you ever lived in Tours?"

Madame Cartier's smile turned to a deep frown. "Why would you ask me that?"

"You remind me of someone I used to know. What about your granddaughter?"

"No, she was born in Royan. She never liked to travel. Not even to Paris." She clutched his arm. "You're certain you won't come to meet her?"

"I'm certain." Gil found her persistence off-putting. Trying not to appear rude, he shook off her grip.

"Suit yourself then," she said and swiveled away from him. When she quickly departed he wasn't too upset.

About half an hour later, the train left for Royan. Peace, at last, he muttered to himself, relaxing undisturbed into his seat.

At 2:45 p.m., Gil arrived in Royan. He grabbed his luggage and approached the taxi stand where a cab driver, around thirty years old, stood by a brown Renault Laguna. The driver smiled at him.

"To the Hôtel Bord du Mer," said Gil. His cousin had made a reservation for him at the beachfront hotel.

Gil handed the driver his luggage. "Do you prefer I sit in the back?"

"As you wish, guy."

Gil sat in front with the driver. As he looked around the city, he thought he could have been in Greece. Many of the city's buildings were white stucco, and their roofs were orange. Tourists easily became lost in these slender streets.

The fee for the taxi ride came to 7.50 euros. Gil handed the driver a ten euro note. "Good day, sir. Keep the change."

The driver's face broke into a wide grin. "Thank you. You are very nice."

"You're welcome."

Gil stepped from the cab and breathed deeply of the sea air. After hours of breathing recycled air on a plane and trains, the fresh air was a blessing.

Reinvigorated, he checked into the hotel. Crisp and clean, its aqua and white color scheme echoed the Bay of Biscay's beach, blue water, and cloudless sky. The front desk and light fixture's reflective surface of the front desk glimmered like a shell's pearly interior.

The front desk clerk handed Gil a note left for him by his cousin, Catherine, telling him to meet her at Conche de Foncillon, one of the city's beaches.

He took his luggage to his room. The room's coastal decor brought a smile to his face. The bathroom offered fluffy white towels, teal- and coral shell-shaped guest soaps, and shampoo the color of seawater.

He stowed a few of his belongings and walked to the beach. The gentle ocean breeze blew through his hair. He passed a crowded swimming pool. Its infinity edge made it appear to blend with the bay. Gil made a mental note to swim there sometime during his stay.

People of various shapes and sizes filled the beach. Families played near the water. Kites dotted the sky, and the air smelled of the ocean, pastries, and delicious meats.

Gil descended the wooden steps leading to the beach. The sand was white, unlike the pebbly beaches he had visited as a child. On spotting his cousin lying face down near a snack shack, he quickened his pace. "Catherine!"

A stunning blonde in a white bikini, it was no surprise she had a starring role in a French police TV series. Her bright blue eyes sparkled at Gil's approach and she stood to wrap him in a tight embrace. He kissed her on both cheeks. "So good to see you again."

"Same here." Catherine returned the kisses. "How was your trip?"

Gil dropped his beach towel on the sand then removed his shorts and dark blue t-shirt. "Had a strange experience on the train."

"Oh?" Catherine dropped back down to her towel and laid her head on her arms. "What happened?"

He told her about his encounter with Madame Cartier. "I found myself wondering if I knew her from my childhood."

Catherine rubbed her forehead. "Valerie Cartier, you said? It's possible. You never forget a face." She straightened and grabbed her beach bag beside her towel. Fishing out her suntan lotion, she smoothed some on her arm.

The orange gel looked and smelled almost edible to Gil. "Do you know her?'

Catherine shrugged. "I can't say I do. It's a fairly common name."

"I asked her if she ever lived in Tours. She didn't seem to want to talk about it," Gil said. "After pestering me about meeting her granddaughter, as soon as I asked about her past she couldn't get away from me fast enough."

Catherine chuckled. "Well, she's long gone. Put it out of your mind."

Their conversation was interrupted by a shout that made them both turn their heads.

A man called out and hastened toward a young woman on the beach.

Gil strained to keep the man in sight. He barely glimpsed the man but thought he might have seen him before.

"Something the matter?" Catherine asked.

"No, why do you ask?"

She shrugged. "You seemed bothered."

"I just didn't like the way that man chased that girl. Something malicious about it. And it's odd to see two people in street clothes on the beach, don't you think?"

"I hardly noticed them." She tapped her temple. "Your little gray cells are working overtime. Relax. You're supposed to be enjoying yourself."

"Thank you for putting me in the same class as the famous fictional detective, Hercule Poirot. Whom we both know is not French. He's—"

"Belgian," they said in unison and laughed.

At that moment, Gil's cell phone rang.

CHAPTER TWO

Gil smiled when he saw the name Jan Barrio on his display. He had been dating her for years. "Hi, Jan."

"Hey babe, you behaving yourself?"

"I am. Catherine and I are enjoying the beach."

"You sound weary."

"It was a long trip, and a little strange." He told her about the elderly lady on the train and the man on the beach who looked familiar. "Anyway, can't wait to see you tomorrow. Love you."

"Love you too."

A glint in the sand caught Gil's eye. He went check it out and passed two young women lounging on the sand. He caught their conversation; they were speaking

German. He studied the language in school for two years but wasn't fluent in it. Hearing a foreign tongue spoken wasn't at all unusual for Royan, home to the highly-regarded language institute, l'École de Langues, which attracted students from nearly 80 countries. He picked up the shell on the beach and returned to Catherine, who lay face down on her towel.

She removed her sunglasses. "What have you got there?"

"Oyster shell. Odd to find it so far from the water. It was next to those two women." He pointed. "They're German, I'm guessing, from the way they talked."

Catherine said. "I speak a little German. Remember, I modeled in Dusseldorf." She sat upright. Upon glancing at the ladies, she stiffened.

Gil touched her arm. "Is something wrong?"

Catherine said, "Let's get out of here." She grabbed her things and shoved them in her bag.

"What's the rush?"

Catherine said, "I've seen those women. Outside of a bar in Toulon. They sold NikNak."

"Knickknacks? What's wrong with that?"

"Not knickknacks. NikNak. It's a form of cocaine, the latest craze. Highly dangerous. It's cut with fentanyl so it's almost immediately addictive."

"You seem to know a lot about it."

"Sorry to say, there's an unfortunate amount of drug abuse in my industry."

"And you believe those two are dealers? No way. Do they know you?"

She shook her head. "At that bar, I thought I'd better not speak to them. I was alone that night. I'd rather not have anything to do with them."

"Say no more. Let's go." Gil tossed the shell aside. "Oysters, mmm. That reminds me. It's been hours since I ate."

"All the more reason to move along. Let's head for Corniche Chay. You'll be glad to know there are several eateries along the way."

Gil tossed on his shirt and shorts. "Sounds good to me." He peered at Catherine. "How come you know so much about cocaine? You don't use any of that stuff, do you?"

"Me? Be serious. But you know. I'm in the entertainment business. It's sad to say but there's a lot of drug use in that world."

At the seaside restaurant, Gil sated his hunger with a platter of breaded fried shrimp and skewered chunks of grilled chicken and beef washed down with an icy Coke.

As they snacked and sipped, a tall, dark-haired man passed by, then doubled back and stopped at their table. He stared at Catherine. "I know you."

She shook her head. "I don't believe so."

"I'm sure of it."

"No, you don't." Catherine's smile was warm but her eyes glowered.

He reached into his jacket and pulled out a small black leather envelope. He flipped it open to display an identification card and badge. "Francois Beaumer. Police. Vos papiers, Madame."

Gil popped up from his seat. "You can't talk to her that way. She hasn't done anything."

"Yours too, young man."

"This is Catherine Robert, a famous actress."

Catherine fumbled in her beach bag and produced her identification.

"So you are," Beaumer muttered. His stern expression softened. "Oh, yes."

"She's the lead character in Deux Fliquettes Marseillaises. That must be why she looks familiar to you."

Beaumer tipped up his chin. "Of course. Yes. And you, young man, do you, uh, work with her?"

"I'm her cousin," Gil said, producing his identification.

His eyes on Gil's documentation, Beaumer asked, of no one in particular, "Do you know a man named George Arnaud?"

"No, I don't," Catherine replied.

The question gave Gil pause but he shook his head.

Beaumer returned Gil's passport. "Thank you for your cooperation," he said, although the set of his shoulders suggested to Gil that he wasn't wholly satisfied. The man started away from the table.

"Officer Beaumer," Gil called. "What do you know about the missing American student?"

Beaumer paused and frowned. "Why do you ask?"

"I was born in Tours but I live in Niagara Falls, New York," Gil replied. "I know of a group of Americans here studying. I'm concerned that the missing student might be someone I know. I'd like to help."

"We appreciate your interest but you needn't involve yourself." He bowed his head. "Enjoy the rest of your day," he said and continued on his way with a couple of backward glances at Catherine.

She shouldered her bag. "Finished?"

Gil nodded. He was ready to move on. The confrontation with Beaumer dampened his spirits. "Does that happen often? Strangers approaching you, I mean."

Catherine laughed. "I hope so. It's an actress's dream to be recognized."

They continued to the next beach. Gil stripped to his swimming trunks. He poked Catherine. "Got any suntan lotion?"

She reached in her bag and squeezed the tube. "Empty."

A stone's-throw away two bikini-clad ladies stretched out on the sand. The huskier one lay face down with her bikini top untied. Her companion said, "I have some if you'd like to borrow it."

"Sure."

She passed him the bottle.

After rubbing suntan lotion on his back, arms, and chest, he handed the bottle back. "Thank you, that was very kind. I'm Gil, by the way. I'm here with my cousin, Catherine."

The lady fastened her top and sat upright. "I'm Mireille. This is Florence." Mireille extended her hand to Gil, who shook it firmly. "You've got some work to do on your tan," she said with a smile.

"I just arrived. Are you from around here?"

Mireille nodded.

"Maybe you could clear up a mystery for me. I met someone on the train. I think I know her from my childhood but can't quite place her." Gil told her about meeting Madame Cartier.

"You're still bothered by that, aren't you?" Catherine said.

"Ah, Valerie Cartier." Florence nodded." I'll bet she tried to fix you up with her granddaughter," said Florence.

Gil rolled his eyes. "How'd you guess? Even when I told her I have a girlfriend, she persisted."

"I've heard other guys complain about the same thing. It's good you gave her the brush off. I know her by reputation. Madame Cartier is a suspicious character. Most people in town don't believe she even has a granddaughter. They've certainly never seen her with one."

Mireille said, "I do hope you two will come to the café where Florence and I work. I think you'll like the food there."

About half an hour later, Gil and Catherine returned to the hotel. They agreed to meet for dinner at seven o'clock. Since he was still suffering from jetlag, he took a two-hour nap.

Around seven o'clock Gil threw on a fresh button-down shirt and a pair of light blue jeans and met Catherine at the hotel restaurant. She wore a blue skirt and a white blouse. He glanced at her feet. She had painted her toenails bright blue, the same color as her eyes.

He winked at her. "You look marvelous."

She kissed him on both cheeks. "So do you, little cousin."

He chuckled. Even though he was now taller than her, she would always refer to him as "her little cousin."

They entered the restaurant arm-in-arm. The restaurant offered an impeccable view of the Atlantic Ocean. He wished Jan could be there with him.

Gil pulled out Catherine's chair. He circled the table to take his seat and nearly collided with another diner.

"I'm sorry. Pardon me." Gil turned to face the woman they had seen at Conche de Foncillon. He muttered a quiet, "Oh, hello."

Catherine glared at the woman.

The woman stepped back. "You're excused. Say, I remember you. From the beach."

"Right," Gil said. "I heard you speaking German, but your French is very good."

The woman smiled at Gil. "Thank you." She looked at Catherine. "Don't I know you?"

"No," Catherine retorted.

"You look so familiar. I work for Lufthansa, the Toulon/Geneva route." She turned to Catherine. "Perhaps I've seen you on one of my flights."

"I couldn't say," said Catherine.

"My name is Greta and my friend is Annalise."

Catherine smiled but it was a forced smile and she said nothing more.

"Well, I'll leave the two of you alone," Greta said, taking the hint. "Maybe you'll join us later at the hotel swimming pool, me and Annalise."

Gil glanced over at Annalise. She was cute, short, and thin with long, blond hair tied behind her head in a French braid. Even from the distance, he could see the freckles that spread from her small nose to her high cheeks accenting her light complexion.

"I'll see," Gil replied. After Greta was out of earshot, Catherine leaned across the table. "I'm telling you, you should avoid those two."

Gil wasn't about to argue. The entire exchange felt off-key as if Catherine and Greta had been talking in code. "You said kept your distance from her in Toulon but she certainly seemed to recognize you."

"It's possible I have flown Lufthansa a few times. Even if I was on one of her flights I would have made an effort not to speak to her."

"One of those celebrity things again," Gil said.

Catherine smiled. "That must be it."

A young, brown-haired waitress approached the table carrying menus. "Something to drink?"

"Apollinaris," replied Gil.

"Une demi-bouteille Chardonnay," said Catherine.

A few minutes later, the waitress brought sparkling mineral water for Gil and a mini-bottle of wine for Catherine. Gil ordered a cucumber salad and haddock, while Catherine chose a tomato salad and rabbit. He patted Catherine's hand. "Hope the rabbit is as good as Grandma's."

Summer Danger

Gil's grandmother often cooked rabbit. It was one of his favorite meals.

"None is better than Grandma's," Catherine replied with a wink.

About an hour later, the waitress returned to ask if they cared for dessert."

"Une marquise au chocolat pour moi," said Gil. He couldn't wait to taste that rich flourless chocolate cake.

The waitress said, "Our desserts are the best in France."

"We'll see about that."

"They are. So, are the two of you local, or are you tourists?"

"I guess you could say I'm a tourist," Gil replied.

She nodded. "I didn't think I'd seen you around. I'm sure you'll find lots to do. Our beaches, of course. Beautiful churches and historic buildings. And plenty of nighttime entertainment. The Monte Carlo is a popular nightspot."

"I'll remember that. Thanks."

The waitress handed the bill to Gil. "Coffee?"

"No, thanks. To Catherine, he said, "We got several suggestions of things to do."

"Yes, but I wouldn't go near that Monte Carlo."

"No? Why not?"

"It's a popular spot for drug-dealing."

Gil narrowed his eyes. "How do you know this? Have you been there?"

Catherine shrugged. "So I hear. Around. You know. Industry gossip."

When she returned with the dessert, the waitress also handed Gil a piece of paper. "My name is Celeste. Here's my phone number." With a wink, she sashayed away.

Catherine shook her head. "Well, well, well. My little cousin has a way with the ladies. First an introduction on the train and tonight, more flirting with you."

Gil glowered. "First of all, I told Madame Cartier I wasn't interested in her granddaughter. And I'm not interested in Greta, Annalise, or Celeste, either. I love Jan."

Catherine laughed. "I was just teasing. So, breakfast, tomorrow?"

"By that time, I'll be hungry again. Eight o'clock too early?"

"No. What would you like to do tomorrow?"

"Visit the cathedral and the market. Maybe swing by the Pentecostal church."

"Oh, okay."

Gil suspected she was trying to be a gracious hostess. He knew Catherine rarely went to church. In Niagara Falls, Gil regularly attended. He kissed

Catherine on both cheeks before retiring to his room. Thinking he ought to be exhausted, he got into bed but couldn't fall asleep. He turned on the television set but found nothing of interest. After walking around the room a while, he decided to go to the pool. Perhaps a swim would help him relax.

Greta and Annalise were in the pool. Annalise's blue eyes sparkled. "You decided to come."

He'd forgotten all about Greta's invitation. "Sure. I like to swim."

"Where is your cousin, by the way?" Greta scanned the pool area.

"She's had enough fun for the day."

"How unfortunate. I looked forward to renewing our acquaintance."

An acquaintance that Catherine denied, Gil thought. He was about to ask for more details when a cell phone rang. Annalise answered the phone and left the pool area, motioning for Greta to join her.

Gil wondered what was so urgent about the call that they left without even saying good-bye.

CHAPTER THREE

Gil returned to his room but still couldn't unwind. Jet lag had his sleep patterns completely off-kilter. Maybe a walk would tire him out enough.

He returned to Corniche Chay and found a whole different world. In the absence of bright yellow sunshine, the beach did not shimmer and the sea did not sparkle. The light of a pallid moon and feeble stars made a lumpy gray blanket of the sand. Lines of ghostly phosphorescence marked waves approaching the shore.

Gil made out three figures in the dark. Two appeared to be Greta and Annalise. They stood in earnest conversation with a man. Had the phone call

Annalise took at the pool been from this man, to set up this meeting? Before Gil could get closer, the man and the two women went their separate ways.

Gil found it disquieting. Catherine said the two women were drug dealers. Had he just witnessed a buy? He would ask Catherine when next he saw her. For now, all he could do was try to put it out of his mind. He walked until he felt tired enough to sleep, left the beach, and returned to his room.

The next morning the ringing of his iWatch alarm jarred him awake. He took a shower and dressed and went downstairs to meet Catherine for breakfast. She was already seated at a table with a teacup, cereal bowl, and grapefruit. Gil kissed her on both cheeks.

Celeste approached the table. "What would you like to drink?"

Gil ordered his favorite hot beverage, hot chocolate. "You were on duty last night. You work some long hours, don't you?"

"Yes, but I do get time off. You said you were a tourist. Maybe I could show you around the city. I really like it here in Royan. I'm sure you will too."

"I'll think about it. My girlfriend arrives here later today. She'd be happy to meet you."

Celeste gave a strained smile. "We'll see about that."

Gil got up from the table and helped himself to scrambled eggs, sausage, roasted tomatoes, and two sourdough rolls from the buffet. What an indulgence, he thought. At home, he rarely had such a feast for breakfast. He murmured a quick blessing for the bounty.

When he returned to the table, he told his cousin about the prior night's event. "Don't you find it odd, people meeting like that on the beach in the middle of the night?"

Catherine shook her head. "You were on the beach in the middle of the night and you're not odd. OK, maybe you are a little bit." She laughed.

"Do you think it had to do with drugs?"

"It's none of your concern, now, is it? Just forget it. You're just as stubborn as Uncle Claude."

"He is one of my favorite people. He'd know what to do about this missing girl."

"As Chief Inspector, I should hope so. And you want to follow in his footsteps, I know. But this isn't even his jurisdiction so don't be bothering him about it." Catherine patted his hand. "Relax. It's police business and you're not a cop yet so there's nothing you can do. Anyway, you're on vacation. When does Jan get here?"

Gil checked his watch and smiled. "Not soon enough."

Gil and Catherine finished their breakfast. As they left the restaurant, Greta and Annalise rushed past them toward the hotel exit. "Catherine, look. It's those two women again. Where are they going in such a hurry?"

"Gil! Honestly, you're not happy unless you're chasing some mystery, are you? Now, wasn't there something you wanted to do today?"

"Well, yes, if you're still up for it."

Half an hour later Gil and Catherine entered the city's noted cathedral. The original structure which dated back to the 1800s was destroyed by World War II bombing as were so many French churches. Reconstructed in the 1950s, the building took three years to complete. An architectural marvel, its concrete V-shaped pillars reached to the sky.

Inside, Gil admired the church's stained glass window. Light filtered through and bathed the nave in a soft, serene luminescence. Gil's pulse slowed and his mind quieted. He felt at peace, transported from petty everyday concerns. The vastness of the space reminded him of God's omnipresence.

Catherine brought him back to earth by asking, "Ready to go?"

He wasn't but she clearly was. "Yes. Thanks for indulging me. I feel refreshed."

"Good. Speaking of refreshment, I could use some. What do you say we stop for a coffee?"

They walked along the street, Gil's head swiveling to take in the shops and businesses along the route: a travel agency, a bank, a restaurant. Ahead, a sleek bright sign indicated a cell phone shop. Gil was dumbfounded by a familiar sight. He noticed first the fluffy Bichon Frisé dog and then by its side, Madame Cartier from the train.

A young man emerged from the store. Madame Cartier stepped into his path. The young man reached down to pet the dog. He straightened and Madame Cartier held something out to him. A few moments later, he smiled and shook his head, and turned to move on. Madame Cartier clutched his arm. Scowling, he pushed her aside and hurried away.

Gil wondered if Madame Cartier had shown the young man her granddaughter's photo and offered to introduce them, as she had proposed to Gil on the train.

Madame Cartier angled toward Gil. Their glances connected. Gil was certain she remembered him from the train. Not only didn't she acknowledge him, but she also did an about-face and darted into the shop.

"Now that's odd," Gil said.

"What?" Catherine asked.

"That was Madame Cartier. The elderly lady from the train. Not only didn't she come over and say 'hello,' she didn't even wave. She seemed surprised—no, shocked to see me."

"Maybe she was surprised to see you in Royan."

"She shouldn't be. I told her this was my destination. That's when she pressed me to meet her granddaughter."

Catherine snorted. "You're worrying too much. You weren't pleased to meet her in the first place." She hooked Gil's elbow. "Come on, the coffee shop's just ahead."

The café was set into the corner of a strip of stores. Striped awnings shaded the wrought iron tables and chairs arrayed on the sidewalk. Gil wondered if this was the shop that inspired "Café de Royan," a famous Pablo Picasso painting. The artwork's vivid primary colors created a vibrant image the captured the seaside city's spirit.

Gil also recognized a face. Seated at one of the tables was Mireille who lent him suntan lotion when he and Catherine were at Corniche Chay. In a white blouse and navy blue skirt with a red scarf around her neck, she looked as if she had stepped out of the Picasso painting. As Gil and Catherine drew near she rose from her chair.

"Is this where you work?" Gil asked.

"Oh, no. I'm on break."

"You get a break and you go to a different coffeehouse? Busman's holiday?"

Mireille laughed. "Care to join me?"

Gil and Catherine took seats.

A waitress about the same age as Mireille came out of the front door and approached the table. "Hello, Mireille. Checking out the competition?"

"Hello, Colette. As espresso for me, please, and cappuccinos for my guests." She turned to Gil and Catherine. "Unless you rather have tea?"

"Coffee for me," Catherine said, and Gil nodded in agreement.

"Do you know every waitress by name?" Gil asked.

"Just about. We servers, we all get off work at about the same time and end up partying at the same clubs. Have you been seeing the sights?" Mireille asked

Gil told her about their visit to the cathedral.

"Oh, good choice. That's a stunning building, inside and out."

"I'm glad I had a chance to see it," Gil said.

Colette arrived with their beverages. Friendly quibbling over who would pay the bill ensued.

Gil didn't know which to tackle first, the creamy-topped coffee or the luscious chocolate-chip pastry that accompanied it. "A curious thing happened after we left the church," he said. "You remember me asking you about Valerie Cartier?"

Mireille nodded.

"We saw her just outside a cell phone store."

"I think I know which one you mean. What of it?"

"She acted like she didn't know me. And then went into the store as if she were avoiding me."

"You're fortunate. Madame Cartier can be annoying. She frequently came to my café. I was aware numerous people didn't like her. She bothered people, trying to get them to come to her home to meet her granddaughter. She was so insistent about it, some people thought it suspicious." Mireille sipped her coffee. "I don't know that anyone ever did go. To her credit, she often left me an extra tip because I knew she liked her Tea Des Poetes. She could well afford it. The woman is filthy rich." She set down her cup. "I should be going. Thank you for the coffee. It was great to see you and I hope we'll meet again." She stood and with a wave set off down the street.

"Catherine?"

Gil looked over his shoulder. A tall man stood behind him smiling at Catherine. The man's height, the way he held himself, struck Gil as familiar but he couldn't place him.

"Pierre," she said but her flat expression told Gil she was not delighted to see this man.

"May I join you?" Without waiting for an answer, he took the chair Mireille had just vacated. Though he held his cigarette off to the side, the smoke reached Gil's nose and overpowered the coffee aroma.

"Pierre, this is my cousin, Gil. Gil, Pierre Desjardins."

Gil and Pierre shook hands.

"Your cousin and dated in Tours," Pierre said.

Catherine's smile was almost a wince and she neither confirmed nor denied it.

"What are you doing in Royan?" he asked.

"Vacationing. With Gil."

"And where are you from?" Pierre asked.

"Originally from Tours," Gil replied. "But I live in New York, now."

"What are you doing in Royan, Pierre?" Catherine asked.

"I have business here. I'm part owner of a club. The Monte Carlo."

"Wasn't that the one Celeste mentioned to us?" Gil asked Catherine. "Celeste is the waitress at our hotel."

Desjardins smiled. "It's great to hear that the locals are talking us up."

Gil didn't mention that the club had a shady reputation. "Since you have a business here, you must know a lot about what's going on in Royan. On my way in I learned about some other visitors, some American students. And one of them is missing. Have you heard anything about that?"

Desjardins shook his head. "Can't say that I have."

With a napkin, Catherine brushed pastry crumbs from her lips. "Ready to go, Gil?"

Gil took that as a cue. "I am. Nice to have met you, Pierre." He had yet to figure out why he detected tension between the man and his cousin.

"And you. I hope to see you at my club."

As they moved down the street, Gil said, "You dated that man?"

Catherine snorted. "He might think they were dates. I thought we were just having drinks."

"Good to know. I don't want to think of my cousin as being involved with a man who owns a club used for drug trafficking."

"Me? Involved? No way," Catherine said but Gil thought her smile somewhat strained.

CHAPTER FOUR

"Where would you like to go next?" Catherine asked.

"The language institute."

Catherine's eyebrows rose. "Why that? Wouldn't you rather visit a museum or one of the historic mansions? Or, go back to the beach?" She winked. "Pretty girls in bikinis?"

"There's a group of American students from my area attending the school. I thought I'd ask around and see if I can connect with them."

"American students ... wait a minute. You're not obsessing about that missing girl?"

Gil glowered. "None of my business, you said. Something for the police to handle, you said."

Catherine nodded. "And yet, you're still brooding about it."

"That policeman, Beaumer? He dismissed it like it wasn't important. Maybe it's nothing but I need to know. You don't have to come. I can catch up with you later."

"Oh, no. I'll come along," was her quick reply. "I do want to spend time with you while you're here."

They continued along the boulevard past shops, restaurants, a park, a stadium. In many ways, the vista was like many other cityscapes but since it was new to Gil it felt different and special.

L'École de Langues came into view. Curving around the trim lawn the sparkling white multistory building seemed to reach out to embrace them with welcoming arms. The wide front walk and low stone steps guided them to the entrance. The lobby's primary colors and the students' animated chattering radiated palpable energy.

The institute offered intensive English, Spanish, and German language programs for school-aged and adult learners as well as French as a foreign language for non-natives. The courses were without a doubt demanding but students had elected to be here. When they did take a break, the beach was a few blocks away. Gil imagined this was a terrific place to study. He found the vitality and drive of so many people intensely pursuing a goal contagious.

He perused the posters and notices lining the corridor walls. Leisure-time, sport, and cultural activities were available for the students when not hard at work. The school helped students find lodgings in hotels and apartments and even placed them with host families.

Catherine regarded the faculty and staff directory.

"Finding something interesting?" Gil asked.

She shrugged. "There's a student lounge down the hall."

"Is that your way of telling me you'd like a soda?"

She grinned.

They stepped into a spacious, high ceilinged room bright with sunlight streaming through plate glass windows. Students sprawled on long white banquets or sat grouped around café tables. The room buzzed with animated conversations in multiple languages. Catherine snagged a table and Gil went to fetch soft drinks. He caught a smattering of German and recalled seeing the two women on the beach during the night.

He brought the beverages to the table, sat, and snapped his fingers. "I've figured it out, why I thought your boyfriend looked familiar."

"My boyfriend?"

"Pierre Desjardins."

Catherine scowled.

Gil shook his head. "Sorry, not 'boyfriend.' Not dates, just drinks. I think he was the man I saw on the beach last night with the German women."

"Are you sure?"

"Not one-hundred percent but he could have been."

"Well, how odd," Catherine murmured.

As he sipped his drink, Gil scanned the room. One student had taken "the French experience" to heart. Wearing a beret, a neckerchief, handlebar mustache, and goatee, he looked like he could have stepped out of a vintage poster.

Gil was startled to spot a familiar face. "Would you believe I see someone I know?" he asked Catherine. "Do you mind if I go over and say 'hello'?"

"Not at all."

Gil strode to a neighboring table. "Jacob Morse?"

A young man with spiky hair and wearing a hoodie sat sipping from a straw. He raised his head. "Gil? Gil Leduc? Is that you?" Jacob stood and held out his hand. "What a surprise. What are you doing here? Are you taking a course?"

Gil shook his head. "Playing tourist. I'm vacationing. I'm spending time with my cousin, Catherine." He pointed to where she sat and waved.

"You remember Hope Becker?" Jacob indicated his tablemate, a younger woman with a fair complexion and auburn hair under a yellow ball cap.

Grinning, Hope rose to hug Gil.

"Of course. How are you two enjoying the program here?"

"It's amazing. I'm learning so much. Soon I'll be able to speak as well as you."

"We were catching our breath before our next class but then we'll take a lunch break. If you don't have other plans, how about you join us?" Jacob said.

"Sounds great."

"Meet us at La Fiesta."

Hope chuckled. "I know that sounds like a Mexican restaurant and you didn't come all the way to France to eat Mexican food. But it's highly rated and known for seafood."

"It's not far from here," Jacob added. "It's across from Conche de Foncillon."

"Let's check with Catherine, OK?" Gil led Jacob and Hope to where Catherine sat, made introductions, and proposed the lunch idea.

"You didn't get enough for breakfast?" Catherine asked.

"Well, I—"

She laughed. "I'm teasing you. Besides, it's not as if we haven't gotten in our fair share of exercise with all the walking we've done. I think I've heard of that place. Sure, let's check it out."

Hope and Jacob departed for their class.

As they exited the student lounge, Gil glimpsed another familiar face.

"Well, if it isn't Madame Cartier," he murmured to Catherine.

"Who?"

"You know, the woman on the train who tried to interest me in her granddaughter. What is she doing here?"

Catherine frowned. "I don't know but we should split before she spots you and decides to pester you again." She hooked his elbow and led him from the lounge.

###

Their destination restaurant couldn't be missed, its name spelled out in tall letters on the topmost level of its sinuous curved façade. Gil spotted Jacob and Hope on the patio seated at counter-height tables under conical white umbrellas.

A young waitress came to take their drink orders. Gil asked if she knew Celeste and Mireille. "They're waitresses at other Royan restaurants."

"Probably," she replied. "We all get off work at the same time and end up at the same clubs."

Gil laughed. "That's what Mireille said."

"If they've been to the Monte Carlo, it's likely we've met." The waitress tapped her order pad with her pen. "I'll get your drinks."

"The Monte Carlo, eh?" "Hope said. "We've been there."

"You have?" Gil said. He glanced at Catherine wondering if he should mention the club's dubious reputation. When she didn't say anything he decided to let it pass for the time being. "I met the man who owns that place," he said instead. "He's Catherine's boy—"

Catherine scowled.

"Acquaintance," Gil finished.

"What a coincidence," Hope said.

The waitress brought their drinks, a kir and a pastis for Hope and Jacob, a mojito for Catherine, and an alcohol-free version for Gil, and took their meal order.

"We were there with Ashley Slick," Jacob said. "Did you know her?"

Gil snapped his fingers. He thought the name sounded familiar when he read about her in the paper. "If I'm thinking of the right person, she was kind of quiet. You don't happen to have a picture of her, do you?"

Jacob shook his head but Hope said, "I think I do." She produced her phone. "I do. Here's a bunch of us at a birthday party. Ashley's fourth from the left. Kind of in the back there, see?"

"Yes, that's her. She is in the French club, isn't she?"

"She is. She is quite the dedicated member. She does a lot of behind-the-scenes work for the club but doesn't make a big fuss out of it, doesn't expect lots of thanks. She traveled here with us. Ashley loves the French language, wants to become fluent in it so she was excited about studying at the institute. Her parents almost didn't let her come. They worried about international terrorism."

"And she's eager to meet a French guy," Hope added with a smile. "She's never had a boyfriend. So she plans to study hard then try out her new conversational skills with a handsome Royannaise."

Jacob said, "I catch her talking to guys on the beach and tease her about it. She says she's just practicing her command of the language but she blushes."

"You should have asked her to come along to lunch," Catherine said.

Jacob frowned. "That's just it, you see. She's missing."

"What's that about?" Gil asked but the conversation ground to a halt with the arrival of their food. He was hard-pressed to decide what was more demanding of his attention, the missing girl or his platter of paupiette de sandre—pike-perch rolls— and cagouilles—land snails—dishes not served in North

American restaurants. The salty tang mingled with the rich aroma of Catherine's crispy grilled goat cheese and the smoky smell of the grilled duck breast Jacob and Hope split.

After everyone dug in and got a few appetite-appeasing bites, Gil asked, "About Ashley. What's this about her being missing?"

"Well, we don't know for sure. It's just that we haven't seen her in class or at the hotel."

"We're all staying at the Hôtel Les Bleuets, across from the Conche de Foncillon," Hope said, snagging a slice of duck with her fork.

"Maybe she met that man of her dreams and ran off with him to 'practice her French,'" Gil said with air quotes.

Hope shook her head. "I suppose she could have gone off exploring but that's not like her. She's studious, serious about keeping up with her assignments. She wouldn't just take off and miss class, not when she worked so hard to get here. We asked the school, the hotel concierge, if she said anything about going away," Hope added. "Negative."

Jacob frowned. "The concierge let us peek into her room. Her clothes are still there, her backpack, too. She carried her passport in it, her money, that sort of thing. It's something of a mystery. I like reading mysteries for fun but I never thought I'd be involved in a real one."

"Gil is something of a sleuth," Catherine said. "He's been bothered about this missing girl ever since he read about it."

"Read about it?" Jacob said. He looked at Hope. "Are you going to eat that last bite?"

"No, you go ahead."

"It was in a newspaper I grabbed in Paris before I got on the train here. A very small article, just a couple of lines mentioning a missing American student, no details other than the name." Gil munched a snail from his platter. "I thought I recognized it. When did you last see her?"

Jacob and Hope tipped up their heads and gazed at the sky as if to find the answer written there.

"At the Monte Carlo, wouldn't you say?" Jacob asked Hope.

She nodded. "Maybe we should ask around there if anyone saw her. She could have left with someone or mentioned where she planned to go. She stuck close to us. At least, when we first got there."

Jacob nodded. "She loosened up after we had been there a while, come to think of it. Quite a lot, actually, considering she's kind of shy. She bounced around on the dance floor, chatted up guys. I'll try to remember what she was drinking. I'll have two of those the next time."

Gil took another bite of shrimp. "Do you go there often?"

Jacob gave him a questioning look. "You ask that as if there's some problem."

"Catherine says there's drug dealing going on there. You haven't noticed anything out-of-place?"

Jacob and Hope shook their heads. "Where did you hear that?" Jacob asked Catherine.

Her focus on her lunch, Catherine replied, "Gossip on the set, between takes."

"Catherine is in a TV show," Gil explained.

"I knew you looked familiar," Jacob said. "We've never noticed anything unusual at the club. In fact, we've even seen teachers and staff members from the institute there."

"Right," said Hope. "Like Mr. De la Rosa. He goes there."

Jacob nodded. "He's not a full-time teacher; he's a tutor. Anyone who needs extra help can hire him."

"De la Rosa," Gil murmured. "I know that name. If I'm not mistaken, he teaches at a Niagara County school."

"I wouldn't be surprised," Jacob said. "He's great. He takes a personal interest in the students he works with. I know Ashley felt comfortable with him. I saw her talking with him at the Monte Carlo."

"It must have been some night for Mr. De la Rosa. He was late to class the next day," Hope said.

"I remember that," Jacob said. "He apologized, mentioned something about running into an old friend from his student days, and lost track of time." Jacob drained his drink. "You're worried about Ashley, aren't you?"

"I didn't know her that well, but, yes, I am," Gil replied. "The police don't seem to be but I plan to keep asking questions until someone puts my mind at ease."

Jacob nodded. "We're worried too. It's not like her. You could come with us to the Monte Carlo. You too, Catherine," Jacob said. "You could find out more than we can. You can ask the owner since he's your boyfr—"

"Acquaintance," Gil said with a nod to Catherine.

"Let me make sure I've got your number," Jacob said. He pulled his phone from his pocket and Hope produced hers as well. They double-checked their contact lists. "Great. We'll let you know the next time we plan to go there."

"Sounds good," Gil said. "I'm glad I ran into you two. By the way, do you know a woman named Valerie Cartier? An older woman."

Jacob pressed his lips together in thought then said, "I think I know who you mean. She hangs out in the lounge. It's weird because if she's a student there, she not in any class that I know of. I've never spoken to her myself. How do you know her?"

Gil gave him a brief report about his encounter with the woman on the train.

"As I said, weird," Jacob replied, "Meanwhile, we better head back to class. Thanks for lunch. It will be our treat next time. Great to meet you, Catherine."

Jacob and Hope set off back toward l'Ecole.

Gil summoned the waitress and asked for the bill.

"Did that satisfy your hunger?" Catherine asked. "For sleuthing as well as food?"

"It's not a joke."

"No, it's not. I'm sorry. I shouldn't have made light of it. I know you're concerned about your friend. It sounds like a lot of people are on the lookout for her. I'm sure she'll be found." She smiled. "Likely you'll find that it was all a misunderstanding."

"I hope so," Gil replied without much confidence."

"Where would you like to go next?"

CHAPTER FIVE

Gil replied. "I should get a map."

"Where do you want to go?"

"Boulevard Georges Clemenceau."

"Why? What's there?"

"The Pentecostal Church. I plan to go there tonight."

"But it's not Sunday."

"They have a midweek Bible study. I'd like to make sure I know the location, familiarize myself with the place so I don't feel like a total stranger later."

"Ah, it's back the way we came," she said. "How about I drive us there? We can digest our lunch while we ride."

"No argument from me," Gil replied, patting his belly. "You're sure you want to come? I know it's not your scene."

"I told you, Little Cousin, I want to spend time with you while you're here."

They got Catherine's gray Peugeot from the hotel parking lot. As they neared their destination address, Gil said, "This is the place." He recognized the church from the pictures he had seen on the church's website. Unlike the cathedral, the church was only one story high and was white with a Spanish tile roof. The gate in front of the church was open.

"I spied a market a few blocks away. I'll go window-shop and meet you back here," said Catherine.

"I won't be long." Gil entered the church's front yard. He strolled around and no one seemed to be about. He circled to the rear and spotted an older man trimming a hedge.

The man approached him. He was short and slender but had a muscular build. His thinning white hair covered only some of his head. He wore dark pants, a white and green plaid shirt, and a blue jacket which he left open. Gil introduced himself, told the man he was in Royan on vacation spending time with his cousin, and that he had discovered the place via the Internet.

Summer Danger

"Welcome. I'm so glad you stopped by. My name is Jacques," the man said. "To look at it now, you might not believe we started in someone's dining room. We have grown large enough to need this space." With a sweep of his arm, he included the building and the grounds. "This was once a warehouse. But we have all lent our talents as carpenters, electricians, plumbers, and so forth to transform it to meet our needs for a meeting place. We still pitch in whatever it takes to maintain it. That's why I'm here today, working in the yard."

"I plan to return this evening. A Bible study is scheduled, am I correct? My girlfriend will be arriving to join me. Is it all right if she comes too?"

"Yes, indeed. We'd be delighted to have you both."

"Great. I'll be back later. Say, have you lived in Royan long?

"Years, young man."

"I met a woman on the train who was also headed for Royan. We had only a brief conversation. Do you know Madame Valerie Cartier?" asked Gil.

Jacques replied, "I do, although I don't know much about her. She's fairly new to Royan, I believe. I understand she lives in a large villa not far from Conche de Foncillon. She has come to our social-room gatherings but I'm sorry to say she was meddlesome, as though she had an ulterior motive for being there. We suspect she was up to no good. In fact, she was asked not to return to our church."

"Why not?"

"After the service one day, she approached one of our young members, determined to get him to visit her and meet her granddaughter. Even when he declined she was insistent. Now, we want to be welcoming and supportive but she made him uncomfortable. I was the lead deacon here at the time. I told the pastor about it. What made you ask?"

"I had a similar experience with her. It struck me as odd."

Jacques nodded. "I think you are wise to be skeptical. It's not for me to spread gossip or speak unkindly of someone I barely know, but—"

"Say no more. I will definitely avoid her. That's not the only strange thing that's happened on my trip." Gil told him about the missing student. "She was last seen at the Monte Carlo. Do you know anything about that place?"

The man said, "I'm sorry about your friend and surprised to learn that. Our city is relatively safe. I've heard of the Monte Carlo but I don't know much about it. I'm not the nightclub type myself."

"I understand. Well, thank you for your time. I'd better be off to connect with my cousin."

"No problem, young man. I hope to see you later."

Summer Danger

Gil set off down the boulevard and spotted Catherine coming to meet him. She pulled to the curb and he climbed in. "What did you find at the market?"

"The market? Oh, it was great. It's mostly a food market: meats, fish, seafood, fruit, vegetables. Everything looked fresh and delicious. I didn't buy anything. After all, we just ate lunch. So, ready to head back to the hotel?"

"There's one more place I want to check out. The Lycee Atlantique."

"That's not far from here. That's a high school. What's of interest to you there?"

"I might learn about Ashley. Maybe she connected with a student on the beach. She might have felt more comfortable with someone younger than the students at the institute."

Catherine propped her hands on her hips. "Gil, seriously! Leave this investigation to the police. They've probably already found out there's nothing to it and you'd be spinning your wheels."

Gil held up his hands in surrender. "You're right."

Catherine sighed with relief. "Good. Jan should be arriving soon. Come on, let's head back."

At their hotel, they changed into beachwear and got comfortable on the sand. Gil messaged Jan with their location. The day's exertions had tired him more than he realized and he fell asleep in the sun. He had a pleasant dream about being tickled then realized real feet rubbed his stomach. He opened his eyes to see three teenage girls wearing cowboy hats standing next to him. "Well, what a surprise." He popped up and pulled Jan toward him.

"Gil, it's been forever," she said, wrapping her arms around him.

He picked her up and twirled her around. "Welcome to France, honey. I never thought this day would arrive." He set her down and kissed her on the lips.

One of her companions shook her head. "Wow, Gil. You act as though you haven't seen her in over a year."

"It does seem like it."

The other young woman crossed her arms over her chest. "Are we chopped liver here?"

Jan said, "All right. You're allowed a hug each."

Gil slipped one arm around both of the other girls. "Welcome, you two. Catherine, let me introduce you. Jan you know, of course. The blond with the streaked hair is Alyssa Rowe and the third Musketeer here is Liz Manuel. Liz worked at the same store I did. Ladies, this is my cousin, Catherine."

Liz's face softened into a smile. "Pleased to meet you, Catherine."

"Liz is in Media like you, Catherine," Gil said.

Liz laughed. "I wouldn't call editing the high school newspaper and hosting a blog being in the same league as a famous actress."

Catherine wiggled her shoulders. "Oh, you have heard of our show even across the Big Pond?"

Liz replied, "Gil can't stop bragging about his celebrity cousin."

"Don't let her kid you, Catherine. Liz is a great writer."

Liz looked around. "It's beautiful here. I like it better than the beaches in Cornwall, England."

Alyssa nodded. "Wow. It really is. Just like the videos on YouTube."

"How was the flight?" Gil asked.

Liz said, "Fine. People were wondering what kind of a weirdo we were with. Alyssa must have drunk a dozen cups of coffee and was bouncing in her seat. I asked a flight attendant to cut her off. She looked at me like I was nuts. At one point I denied knowing her."

Alyssa waved her hands. "Like, I only wanted to have fun. Couldn't help laughing. Some friend you are."

Jan frowned. "Hey, knock it off, you two. I've listened to enough of your nonsense."

The girls placed their towels down by Gil. Liz and Alyssa removed their t-shirts, revealing the bikinis they wore underneath, and brought out softball gloves from their beach bags.

Gil groaned. "Come on. Not in France."

Alyssa lifted her brows. "We've got a tournament to play in. We need to stay in practice."

Jan said, "Alyssa's right. This might be all fun and games for you, but some of us have lives." The three girls played on their high school softball team as well as a summer league team.

Gil wondered if ferreting the whereabouts of a missing student and exploring the background of a strange older woman who showed up everywhere he went counted as "fun and games" in anyone's book but his.

Jan removed her shorts. "Buddy, let's take a walk. I need some alone time with you."

Gil grabbed her hand and walked with her toward the ocean.

Jan said, "You seem like you've got something on your mind."

"You could say that." Gil brought her up to speed on the two mysteries. "When I first read about the missing student, I was concerned for a moment it could be one of your crew. It's not but—" He threw up his hands. "No, I'm not talking about it anymore. I told Catherine I'd leave it alone."

"That hasn't stopped you from worrying though, has it? I'll bet you've been investigating."

"The police here don't seem to be doing anything." He threw an arm around Jan's shoulders and pulled her close. "Now that you're here, I'd make better progress. It's like Sherlock has got his Watson."

She frowned at him. "And who's Sherlock and who's Watson?"

He clasped her shoulders. "I'm sure sleuthing around Royan isn't what you had in mind for a vacation. I promise, not another word."

"Are you kidding? Who helped you solve the Purity Ring murders?" She bopped him on the biceps. "I just want to spend time with you, buddy."

Gil laughed. "That's what Catherine said."

"And here we've deserted your cousin and left her with my crazy friends. C'mon, let's rescue her."

Alyssa and Liz were sprawled out on beach towels.

"Hey, I've got an idea," Alyssa said. "Like, are you all up for clubbing tonight?"

"Clubbing?" Catherine echoed.

"Alyssa loves to dance," Gil said.

"Our cab driver told us about a popular spot. We should go check it out. The Monte Carlo."

"I don't know," Gil said. "I've heard some negative things about that place. Right, Catherine?"

His cousin nodded.

"Negative?" Jan asked. "Such as?"

"Drug trafficking."

Alyssa frowned. "You don't say? How do you know that, Catherine? Do you live here?"

Catherine shook her head. "I came down from Tours to be with Gil. But, I hear things. There is an unfortunate amount of drug use in my industry and word gets around."

Gil added, "And I intended to go to a Bible study tonight. Jan, if you don't have plans with your friends …"

"I'd be interested to see how that's done in a church here," she said.

"Oh." Alyssa pouted.

"Tell you what. How about we all go to the Monte Carlo tomorrow night? Safety in numbers?"

Liz nodded. "Good idea. Come to think of it, we should probably get an early night, Alyssa. That way jet lag won't have us dragging around all day tomorrow."

"I'll pass too. I should check in with my agent," Catherine said. "We need to talk about the show's next season. Jan, it looks like you've got Gil all to yourself."

###

That evening, Gil and Jan arrived at the Pentecostal Church. Jacques introduced them to Gisele, his wife. She clasped Gil's hands. "Jacques told me about your meeting earlier today."

"He was very welcoming. We had a nice chat."

"Please, sit with us," she said.

The session opened with prayer followed by singing to warm the spirit and open the heart. After the congregation sang, the man who led the singing, said, "Tonight we have visitors from the other side of the Atlantic and I would like for one of them to tell me about his or her relationship with Christ. If either wants to?"

Without thinking, Gil said "I will" and stood then realized he didn't know what to say. He offered a brief prayer asking for wisdom and inspiration. He faced the congregation of about twenty-five people and spoke about how as a five-year-old he was disappointed to learn he would move to America. If he had not moved there, however, he would have never met Jan and her family and several people who had become his friends. His grandfather had told him how God's plans are often not our plans, but His way is the better way.

Gil took his seat, relieved when a few people clapped.

A few minutes later, the deacon launched into a sermon on the healings of Jesus. A noise at the back of the sanctuary drew Gil's attention. He glanced over this shoulder to see Pierre Desjardins. Gil whipped his head back to face front, hoping he hadn't been spotted. "What is he doing here?" he muttered.

"Who?" Jan whispered.

"Tell you later," Gil replied, not wanting to disrupt the sermon.

When it ended, Gil turned just in time to see Desjardins dash for the exit. Gil made it to the front door in time to see Desjardins speed down the street in a red Citroen. Gil could catch only the first two digits of the license plate. Fuming, Gil reentered the church. "He got away."

"Who?" Jan asked again.

"Someone Catherine knows." Gil explained about meeting Desjardins at the Café Picasso.

Jacques touched Gil's arm. "You okay, Gil?"

"I spotted someone I don't feel right about," Gil said. He described Desjardins. "Has he been here before?"

"I can't say that he has."

"It just seems strange that he'd be here." Gil didn't want to say it but he felt as if he were being followed.

Jacques shrugged, "The study was open to visitors. It is curious he didn't stay. I can see you're uneasy about it."

Gisele said, "Why don't we take you back to your hotel tonight. Where are you staying?"

"Hôtel Bord du Mer," said Gil.

Jacques said, "On Allés Les Roches?"

"That's right."

A few minutes later, Gil and Jan got out of Jacques's green Audi. They told them they planned to be in church on Sunday.

The youths entered the hotel. Gil wrapped his arm around Jan. "Are you hungry?"

Summer Danger

Jan said, "Sure am. Haven't eaten since we got here."

They entered the restaurant and Celeste came to greet them. She pointed at Jan. "Let me guess. You're Gil's girlfriend."

Jan said, "Yes, I'm Jan."

"Oh." Celeste led them to a table without saying another word.

After the waitress departed, Gil said, "She was friendlier last night when I was with Catherine."

Celeste returned to take their drink order and Gil ordered two small bottles of Perrier.

When Celeste returned with the water and poured their drinks, Gil said, "One question, please."

"Sure." Celeste flashed him a flirtatious smile.

"When I was here with my cousin, did you notice the woman I bumped into? I'm wondering if you've seen her before"

Celeste frowned. "Yes, she's a guest here. She and another woman. You sure are inquisitive."

Jan shook her head. "Don't worry. He's always like this."

Celeste said, "Well, better than a guy who won't talk. I've been out with such guys. Needless to say, there was no date number two. I believe the two women are flight attendants."

"You don't say. Interesting," Gil drawled.

After Celeste left the table, Jan grabbed Gil's hand. "What's this all about? Asking about other girls?"

Gil detected fire in his girlfriend's green eyes. Although few people were in the restaurant, Gil lowered his voice. "My first day here when I was at the beach, two women were speaking German. They seemed certain they knew Catherine but she said they weren't acquainted. She thought they might be drug dealers."

Jan raised her eyebrows. "A missing student, a strange older woman, a friend of your cousin's who's trailing you, and now two mysterious German women."

"I was hoping to have a relaxing vacation with Catherine and you."

She narrowed her eyes. "You're not giving up on any of it, are you?"

Gil gave her an apologetic smile.

"Well, try to put these questions out of your mind for tonight. Let's enjoy our dinner." She pointed to the menu. "What looks good here?"

Gil winked at her. "Salad and wild rice with rabbit and mushrooms."

Jan wrinkled her nose. "What? You want me to eat Peter Cottontail?"

"Come on. It tastes like chicken. I know you love chicken."

"Just teasing you."

Celeste took their orders. Both Gil and Jan ordered rabbit and salad.

Liz and Alyssa approached the table. Liz smiled. "May we join you?"

Gil frowned. "I don't know. We already ordered."

Jan dismissed Gil with a wave. "Don't listen to him. Of course, you may."

Gil shook his head. "I was only kidding."

"Get enough sleep, ladies?" asked Jan.

Liz said, "I think so. Now I'm almost as perky as Alyssa."

Alyssa said, "I couldn't sleep. I'll probably be up all night."

"That's what you get for drinking so much coffee."

Alyssa touched Gil's arm. "You're the expert on local cuisine. Like, what do you recommend?"

"Rabbit and salad."

Alyssa wrinkled her nose. "Yuck."

Jan pointed her fork at Gil. "Well, Lover Boy claims it tastes just like chicken."

"It does!" insisted Gil. "It's a very popular dish here."

Celeste approached the table. "What would you ladies like to drink and eat?"

Alyssa said, "The same thing they're eating."

Celeste returned with the beverages. She tilted her head at Gil. "Where's the woman you were with last night?"

"She had business to attend to."

"Perhaps she would like a meal sent up to her room," Celeste said.

"That's a great idea. Thanks for the suggestion." Gil pulled out his phone and dialed Catherine. He frowned. "That's odd. It went straight to voicemail. You'd think if she was talking to her agent she would at least answer to tell me to try again later."

CHAPTER SIX

Liz shrugged. "Maybe she's on an important call that can't be disturbed."

Celeste brought the dinners to the table. After Alyssa bit into her food, she patted Gil on the shoulder. "You're right. It is good."

Liz said, "I second the motion."

At that moment, Desjardins approached the table. Gil's heart raced.

"Well, hello, Gil. Nice to see you again."

"I tried to greet you a while ago at the church but you took off in such a hurry." Gil tried to contain his pique but something about Desjardins rubbed him the wrong way. What was the man doing here, anyway?

"Did you? I, uh, was there to meet someone. Or thought I was. I didn't see the person I was looking for and figured I was in the wrong place so I left." Desjardins scanned Gil's tablemates. "Catherine not with you?"

"No, these are friends from the U.S."

"Ah, world travelers. Welcome to France, ladies. I don't know what you've got lined up for your visit but I would like to invite you to the Monte Carlo. It's a popular disco and I'm not saying that simply because I am part owner."

Alyssa bounced in her chair. "Like, we were just talking about going there. It's in our plans for sure."

"I'll look forward to seeing you." With a smile and a bow, Desjardins departed.

"Did you hear that?" Alyssa said. "The owner himself invited us. Now we have to go."

"Simmer down, girl," Liz said. "We just got here."

Celeste came to clear the table and ask about dessert.

Liz patted her stomach. "I think I'm too full."

Celeste pouted. "Oh, you really must try one of our desserts. Our pastries are the best in France. I can bring you a plate of macarons. They are meringue-based cookies, pretty and sweet. Did you know, the recipe dates back to the Renaissance? A light treat to polish off your meal. And coffee?"

"No coffee for Alyssa," Liz said which earned her an elbow in the ribs from her friend.

The macarons arrived as small round sandwich cookies in pastel colors. After tentative first bites, the plate was quickly emptied.

Alyssa yawned. "I'm ready to call it a day. Or night. Like, jet lag caught up with me. I have no idea what time it is. How about you ladies?"

Liz nodded but Jan said, "I'm too wired to sleep."

"How about we take a little stroll on the beach? That might help you to unwind."

Jan nodded. Gil and Jan bid the other girls good night and set out. Twilight hadn't yielded to the night and a warm soft summer breeze provided a gentle caress. They drifted away from the beach and reached a well-traveled avenue. Noise, laughter, and music flowed out as people drifted in and out of lodgings, cafes, and restaurants. Lights from street-side balconies washed the pavement. Gil stopped short.

"What?" Jan asked.

"Up ahead. Hôtel Les Bleuets. This is where Jacob and Hope are staying."

Dwarfed by neighboring high-rises, the hotel was only three stories tall and lacked an imposing facade. It did however offer its guests the advantage of being across the road from the beach.

"Jacob and Hope?"

"American students at the language institute. Catherine and I met them this morning."

Jan nodded. "Did you want to stop and say hello?"

"You wouldn't mind?"

"Not at all."

They stepped into the lobby.

"Oh, isn't that clever," Jan said, tilting her head at the front desk which looked like someone had moored a bright blue skiff in the lobby. Gil approached the concierge and asked about Hope and Jacob.

"Oh, yes, I know who you mean. They're out at the moment. Did you want to leave a message?"

"No, thank you. I've got their phone numbers. I'll catch up with them later. But what can you tell me about Ashley Slick?"

"Ah, I get it," Jan murmured.

The concierge grimaced. "I wish I had something to share. We've enjoyed having her as a guest. She's been no problem at all. We are all mystified here. She vanished without a word and no one has a clue."

"Well, thank you," Gil said.

He took Jan's arm and led her back out to the street.

"Ashley Slick? That's the missing girl you told me about."

"It's so strange. From what I've learned about her, she wasn't the type to simply take off and not tell anyone." He sighed. "Want to turn back?"

"Good idea. I'm finally running out of steam. I may end up sleeping until noon."

They had no sooner begun the return trip when Jan said, "Ouch! Silly me, I think I've given myself a blister."

"Let's get you off your feet," Gil said and helped her limp over to a park bench flanked by two trees and surrounded by foliage. "Wait here. I'll ask the concierge if he has a bandage." He circled the herbaceous border to return to the hotel's entrance and stopped.

"Gil? Gil, what are you doing?"

He knelt, plunged into foliage then stood.

"Gil? I don't like the look on your face. What's wrong?"

"I think I've found Ashley."

###

Gil paced in front of the bench where Jan doctored her foot while they waited for the police. Across the road, the concierge darted out onto the sidewalk then back inside like whack-a-mole.

An officer arrived in response to Gil's call. He wore blue shorts and a blue tee-shirt, "police municipale" emblazoned on the back in large white letters, and Gil gathered he'd been called away from his usual duty of patrolling the beach. Gil showed him where the body lay and assured him he hadn't touched it or moved it.

The officer told Gil and Jan to stay put and called for assistance which didn't surprise Gil. An investigation required an officer who was a member of the judicial branch and had more authority.

Standing at parade rest, the policeman moved only when it appeared that passers-by would encroach on the scene.

A plain dark car advanced down the street and came to a stop in front of the hotel. A dark-haired man got out, strode into the lobby, and a few minutes later emerged, the concierge at his side. The concierge pointed to Gil and Jan.

As the man moved into the light, Gil saw it was Francois Beaumer, the officer that had questioned him and Catherine on the beach.

The municipal officer straightened at Beaumer's approach. "Sir, this is the gentleman who reported finding the body."

"Thank you, Officer. I can take it from here."

The municipal policeman gave Beaumer a crisp salute and struck off toward the beach.

"You two," Beaumer said to Gil and Jan, "if you would please remain here for the moment, I have questions I want to ask." Beaumer gave Ashley's body a cursory examination then used his cell phone to make a call. Gil assumed he was summoning crime scene technicians.

Beaumer turned and faced Gil. "You again? Are you staying in this hotel?"

"You know him?" Jan hissed.

"We've met," Gil replied. To Beaumer he said, "No, I'm at the Hôtel Bord du Mer."

"Where Catherine is staying."

"Yes," Gil said, wondering how he knew that. "My girlfriend and I were taking a walk."

"We were just on our way back," Jan said.

"And you stopped to find a body," Beaumer said to Gil with an aside to Jan, "Troublemaker, is he?"

Jan jumped to her feet and sputtered, "Gil doesn't create problems. Quite the opposite, he solves them."

"Does he? And you are …?"

"Jan Barrio."

"Your papers, please."

Jan looked at him. "I don't know what you …"

Gil whispered, "He means your ID, your passport."

Jan reached in her money belt. "Here you go."

"Ah, another American. Your reasons for being in Royan?"

"I'm on vacation. I'm visiting my boyfriend. Is that a crime?"

Jan wasn't usually so confrontational. Gil could tell from the strain in her voice that she was weary and upset. That they had found themselves at a death scene in the past didn't make it any easier this time.

"No, but this certainly seems to be. Tell me how you came to discover this."

"We had stopped at the Hôtel Les Bleuets to ... visit some friends." He itched to call them and tell them Ashley had been found. Catherine, too. But that would have to wait. "They weren't in so we decided to go back to our hotel. Jan sat to check a blister on her foot. I was headed over to the concierge to ask for a bandage—"

Jan waved the paper packaging from the bandage.

"When I spotted something that seemed out of place under the brush. I bent down for a better look and that's when I saw it was Ashley."

Beaumer's eyes narrowed. "Ashley?"

"Ashley Slick. The missing student. The one I asked you about when we met on the beach. You said you didn't know anything about it."

"And you do? You know the victim?"

"We were acquainted back in the States."

A white van pulled up behind Beaumer's car. Two people in white coveralls emerged. Beaumer waved them over. "Stay here," he said to Gil and Jan. "I'll return in a moment." He met the other two officers for a brief conference. They set to work investigating the crime scene and Beaumer rejoined Gil and Jan. He pulled a small notebook from his jacket pocket. "I'm going to want to know more about the victim and your relationship with her. Tell me what room you're in at the Hôtel Bord du Mer. I also want your cell phone number."

Gil provided him the information he requested.

"When we spoke the other day, you were interested in a group of students who traveled here. Was the victim part of that group?"

"She was."

"And do you know the other members of the group?"

Gil didn't want to drag Hope and Jacob into the mess but the truth would come out sooner or later and lying would only add to the suspicions Beaumer already harbored about Gil. "Hope Becker and Jacob Morse. They're staying here too." Gil pointed to the hotel where another police car slowed to find a place to park.

"The friends you were going to meet?"

Gil nodded. "But they're not here. So the concierge told us." Gil felt cold as he realized that made the two students appear questionable.

"Do you have a way to contact them?"

With reluctance, Gil shared their cell phone numbers.

"And your cousin, Catherine Robert, does she know them as well?"

"Catherine? What's she got to do with this?" Jan asked.

Beaumer didn't reply. "Answer the question, please," he said to Gil.

"She met them earlier today but didn't know them before that." Had that been only this morning? Suddenly the day seemed longer than twenty-four hours.

"You're certain of that?"

What kind of question is that? Gil wanted to ask but bit his tongue. "I am," he replied instead. Where was Catherine, anyway?

Beaumer flipped his notebook closed and tucked it away. He withdrew two business cards and handed one each to Gil and Jan. "I'll be in touch. Do not leave the city without contacting me first. You're free to go for now. I'll be in touch but don't hesitate to contact me if you think of anything else that will be helpful." He set off to join the other officers.

Gil stomped along the sidewalk.

"Gil, slow down," Jan cried.

Gil turned to see her limp toward him. "I'm sorry. I forgot about your foot."

"What's your hurry?" she asked.

"I want to get a hold of Hope and Jacob before Beaumer calls them. With any luck, he'll be busy with the crime scene technicians for a few minutes anyway." As soon as they were out of earshot he pulled out his phone and dialed Jacob. The phone rang then went to voicemail. He got the same result when he called Hope. "Where are they?" he murmured. Next, he tried Catherine but she didn't answer her mobile or her hotel room phone. "Hmph," he grumbled and he stowed his phone. He turned to Jan. "How's the foot? Are you OK to keep walking?"

"Oh, sure. The bandage helps. Thanks for getting that. Are you OK? You just found the body of someone you know."

"It wouldn't be the first time," Gil muttered.

Jan clasped his shoulders and turned him to face her. "Talk to me, buddy."

He shook his head. "I had a feeling this was going to end badly."

"I take it you couldn't tell what happened to Ashley."

"No. Whatever it was, I doubt it was a natural death. I didn't get a good look and I certainly didn't want to contaminate the scene in case it wasn't. The light wasn't strong. Something appeared to be smeared on her face, around her nose, but I couldn't tell for sure. Isn't it strange that she's been within yards of the hotel all this time and with all the people who were searching for her, no one found her?"

Jan shrugged. "Shouldn't the hotel groundskeeper have found her?"

Gil replied, "She wasn't on their property. We were in a public park. I suppose eventually a maintenance worker would have discovered her."

They reached their hotel and Jan said, "I'm going to call it a night."

"I'm not surprised. Come one, I'll see you to your room. I'm so sorry. This was not what I had in mind for your first day in France."

Jan kissed him on the cheek. "Don't worry about it, buddy. I hope the police find out what happened. Because if they don't, I know someone who will." She winked.

Gil chuckled. "You know me too well, Jan Barrio," he said and gave her a proper goodnight kiss.

He waited until she entered her room and closed the door then tried Catherine's numbers. When he still got no answer, he tried knocking on her room door but got no response. Reluctantly he went to bed. His body was weary but his thoughts raced like a hamster on an exercise wheel. What had happened to Ashley? And where was Catherine? He prayed he hadn't discovered one missing person only to have another disappear.

CHAPTER SEVEN

Gil woke groggy and cranky. He couldn't decide whom to call first. Jan said she might want to sleep in but he was eager to connect with Hope or Jacob, not to mention Catherine. He tried his cousin's room phone and got no answer. His pulse racing with anxiety, he dialed her cell phone number and breathed a sigh of relief when she answered.

"I'm down at breakfast," she said.

"I'll get cleaned up and join you," he replied.

She was already seated at a table with the same light breakfast as before.

Gil kissed her on both cheeks and eyed her meal. "With all the food on the buffet, that's all you're going to have?"

She patted her midriff. "I have to watch my figure or they're likely to write me out of the show."

Celeste approached the table. "Well, good morning. Where's your girlfriend?"

"Catching up on her jet lag," Gil replied. "Thanks for asking.

"I brought you a hot chocolate but of course if that's not what you want—"

"I'll take it," Gil said. The sweet beverage might improve his mood and spark some energy.

"And I see you're reliving your childhood," Catherine said.

Gil gave her a weak smile. "When in France…? I admit, hot chocolate for breakfast is a favorite memory. You work some long hours, don't you?"

Catherine rolled her eyes. "I thought that call would never end."

Not looking up from his beverage Gill said, "I tried calling you during dinner to see if you wanted room service. Then I tried later that evening. The call went to voicemail, both times."

"Ah, yes, I'm sorry. I'd had the phone set so I wouldn't be disturbed. Otherwise, I'd still be on that call."

Gil struggled to keep his voice level. "I tried your room phone. I went to your room and knocked on the door but you didn't answer."

"After we finally finished, I went for a walk to unwind." She narrowed her eyes. "What was so urgent?"

Gil took a bolstering swallow of chocolate. "Ashley Slick, that missing girl? She's dead."

Catherine laid down her spoon. "Dead?"

"I found her body."

Catherine reached across the table and took both of Gil's hands in hers. "No. Oh, Gil, I'm so sorry. How awful for you. What was the cause?"

"I don't know." Gil described finding the body under a hedge in the park across from the hotel. "It wasn't a natural death, I'm pretty sure of that. An accident, or something worse? I called the police. You won't believe who came to investigate."

Catherine frowned.

"Francois Beaumer. The one who rousted you on the beach the first day I arrived. The one who said he knew you."

"Oh, well, he is a detective. If it looked like a suspicious death …"

"It did. He gave me his card. I'll call him later. Not that he'll tell me anything."

"Do Hope and Jacob know?"

"Maybe. I don't know. I tried to call them last night too but couldn't get through." Gil glanced at his watch. "Maybe it's late enough that I won't risk waking them. Do you mind …?"

"No, go ahead. I'll get you something to eat. Anything in particular?"

Gil shrugged.

"How about some of everything?" Catherine said with a wink and left for the buffet.

Gil tried Jacob's number first and this time the student answered. "Jacob, I tried to reach you last night. Did you hear about—?"

"Ashley? Yeah, the cops got a hold of us, me and Hope. They kept us for hours asking questions. They wanted the specifics of who we are, every minute of our trip, why we're here, what we've done, and where we've been since arrived. They couldn't have asked to know more about us if they demanded a blow-by-blow description of our birth. But would they tell us a thing? No. I'm steamed and Hope is still upset."

"Are you in class?"

"No, we're at the hotel. Neither of us can concentrate."

Catherine returned from the buffet. "Traditional French breakfast," she said and offered him a plate with thin slices of French bread, croissants, and small pots of assorted jams.

"Hold on a minute, Jacob," Gil said.

He brought Catherine up to speed. She gestured at his phone and he handed it over.

"Jacob, it's Catherine, Gil's cousin. I know just what you and Hope need. Why don't you get yourselves out of that room and meet us at Le Doux Secret? It's halfway down the block from your hotel and across the street."

Jacob agreed and Catherine returned the phone to Gil. "Let's go. We have a rendezvous."

Gil looked at the plate of baked goods and pouted.

"Never fear, Little Cousin. There's more where that came from."

On the way out, Gil left a request with the concierge. "If you see Jan or her friend out and about, tell them to give me a call."

Gil and Catherine had a slightly longer walk so Jacob and Hope were waiting for them when they arrived. Gil could tell they'd had a rough night. Jacob's eyes bore dark shadows and Hope's were red.

Catherine hugged Hope's shoulders. "I can see you're worn out. Allow me to order for you."

Hope, Jacob, and Gil took seats on the cafe's deck overlooking the beach while Catherine met the waitress halfway.

"I should apologize, Gil," Jacob said. "I should have called you to tell you about Ashley. But the detective kept us so busy and by the time he left it was the middle of the night and we were worn out."

"No apology necessary," Gil replied. "I knew about it. I found her.

Hope's mouth dropped open and Jacob's eyebrows flew up.

"I tried to call you but all I got was voicemail. And it wasn't the kind of message I wanted to leave."

"We were in the library so of course, we had our phones turned off."

Catherine arrived at the table followed by a waitress bearing a tray.

"You have all had a shock," Catherine said. "Have some herb tea—no caffeine, that will only make you jumpy. And sweet pastries. Sugar will help."

The waitress poured out cups of tea. Hope took a polite sip. A smile tweaked the corners of her mouth and she drank more. Having missed breakfast, Gil helped himself to a bite of croissant. Just beyond the deck, waves rhythmically washed ashore, soothing him as he imagined the stresses of the last couple of days flowing out with the tide.

He filled in Hope and Jacob about finding Ashley's body.

"So she ... died ... right there in front of our hotel?" Hope asked.

"Almost as if she was just leaving or just getting back," Jacob added. "The cop wouldn't even tell us how it happened. Do you have any idea?"

"It was dark and I didn't want to disturb anything so I couldn't see much. It's possible she got hit by a car trying to cross the street to get to or from the beach but I couldn't make out any obvious injuries. I spotted what I thought was discoloration around her nose."

Catherine said, "You didn't mention that earlier."

"It could also have been shadows."

They fell silent, sipping tea and munching pastries. As regularly as the surf reached the shore, beachgoers arrived to spend a day in the sun, spreading towels on the sand and setting up blue-and-white striped umbrellas and cabanas. Laughter, shouting, and music drowned out the sound of the surf.

"You say you were questioned about your trip here?" Gil asked.

Jacob's face flushed. "Almost as if we were suspects. As if Ashley were a suspect."

"Suspect of what?" Catherine wanted to know.

"I have no idea."

Hope said, "I told them we arrived at the airport, we handed over our luggage … Neither of us had much. One case each to check and a carry-on. We went through Security, we got on the plane. Nothing unusual."

"Who was this detective, anyway?"

"Boomer? Beemer? Something like that."

"Beaumer," Gil said. "Francois Beaumer."

Jacob snapped his fingers. "That's it. Say, do you know him?"

"He was the one who responded to the scene last night." Jacob's question was a good one. What suspicions could the detective have of the students? "And the last time you saw Ashley was that night at the Monte Carlo?" Gil asked.

Jacob and Hope nodded.

"Did anything unusual happen?" Catherine asked.

Hope and Jacob exchanged questioning looks and shook their heads.

"It was just, you know, a night at the club. We saw a lot of people we knew. People from school. Even some teachers. That tutor, Mr. De la Rosa, was one. We've seen him there before." Jacob chuckled. "I guess he's not all work and no play." He rubbed his chin. "In fact, I also saw the woman you asked me about, Madame Cartier."

"Oh?" Gil said.

"The detective asked if Ashley was depressed or upset that night but it was just the opposite. You know Ashley. Kind of the quiet type. But she was in high spirits. I've never seen her so excited. I was pleased because I was feeling bad about her being there. A club like that isn't really her scene. I was afraid she went along because we pressured her into joining us." Jacob's expression soured. "We won't be going back for a while. The detective told us to stay away."

"All the more reason to check it out," Gil realized he'd voiced the thought when Jacob said, "I agree. Are you up for going tonight?"

"Let me check with Jan." Gil explained he wanted to spend time with his girlfriend while she was in Royan.

"Understood," Jacob said.

Hope set her teacup in its saucer. "Thank you, Catherine. I do feel better now. Settled."

Catherine grinned. "Shock can lower your blood sugar, so a bit of sweet will help bring that back to normal levels. And the tea is a special nervine blend. I use it myself. Sometimes when we're in production I get so cranked up I can't unwind and get to sleep."

"Sleep sounds like a good idea." Hope stifled a yawn with her hand. "I'd better rest up if we're going out tonight."

"Come on. I'll walk you back," Jacob said. "Gil, let us know about the Monte Carlo, OK?"

Thanking Catherine for the food and drink, Jacob and Hope set off for their hotel.

"I wonder what Beaumer has on his mind," Gil mused.

Catherine frowned. "I'm afraid you'll find out. It sounds like he thinks you're part of the puzzle."

"I'm not, you know. I'm as baffled as everyone else." He munched the last bite of chocolatine. "Well, let's go see if Jan and her friends are awake."

As they walked to their hotel, Gil took a call from Jan.

"Hi, buddy. We've rejoined the world and we're now all on local time. Where are you? Are you OK? I mean, after last night and all."

He was even less OK after talking with Jacob and Hope but that wasn't anything he wanted to share on the phone. "I'm with Catherine. We went for breakfast. We would have called you but we didn't want to disturb you while you were catching up on your sleep."

"We're up now and catching some rays. Look for us on the beach, OK?"

Catherine excused herself to review the material her agent sent. Gil scoured the beach and at last, found Jan and her friends.

Liz and Alyssa heaped him with sympathy. "Jan told us what happened last night. What a way to end the evening," Liz said.

"Try to put it out of your mind. It's such a beautiful day," Alyssa added.

"It is," Gil said, although something Jacob mentioned nagged him. It was about Madame Cartier being at the Monte Carlo. She seemed out of place in the language institute student lounge and even more so at a night club. He seemed to be running into her everywhere: on the train, in front of a shop on the boulevard, and she had even been at the church. Gil couldn't put together a picture that made sense.

Jacques at the church mentioned the woman was wealthy and lived in an expensive villa. Across the bay, upscale residences, some from the Belle Epoque era, lined the road curving around the Grande Conche. "I wonder …" Gil murmured.

"Wonder what?" Jan asked.

"If you'd be up for another stroll."

"If you promise no dead bodies on this one."

"I'll do my best. Ladies, be sure to use sunscreen. You don't need to get an entire vacation's tan in one morning."

"Got it!" Liz said, waving a tube of lotion.

"Come on, I'll show you how the other half lives," Gil said. Hand in hand, he and Jan circled the bay.

Jan let out a whistle. "Oh, I see what you mean. These homes are stunning."

"No argument there." A variety of architectural styles was represented. Some of the mansions were sleekly modern while others were fanciful and ornate, with turrets and cupolas, gables, louvered shutters, and balconies." I should have said how the other half lived, past tense. Some of these are still private residences, but many have been converted into boutique hotels and bed-and-breakfasts."

"I imagine the upkeep was too costly. We saw a lot of that in England where the great halls are now commercial properties." She pointed. "Look at that one, the way it's painted and ornamented. Stripes and checks and polka-dots. It's so whimsical, it makes me think of Alice in Wonderland."

The home a few doors down stood in contrast. A single story, streamlined and contemporary, it was L-shaped, with two wings at right angles to each other. Just as Gil was about to look away, the garage door opened. A dark sedan turned off the road and pulled up the driveway but before it disappeared into the garage, Gil made out the occupants. The driver was Madame Cartier herself, the passenger a young man Gil thought he might have seen in the institute's student lounge when he visited Hope and Jacob. Garbed in beret and neckerchief he was hard to mistake for anyone else.

"Ha!" Gil cried. "I know where you live."

Her brow furrowed, Jan said, "What are you talking about?"

"Madame Cartier. That's her house."

"The older woman you met on the train, the one you thought was a pest?"

"That's the one. Well, what do you say we head back and make sure your friends haven't fried to a crisp?"

Jan linked her elbow with Gil's. They had taken only a few steps when another car came down the street and turned into Madame Cartier's driveway. Gil whipped around in time to see a man get out and approach the front door. It opened and he stepped inside.

"I'd swear I know that man," Gil said.

"What man?"

"The one who just went into Madame Cartier's house." Gil raked his memories for a clue to man's identity. The car he drove gave a hint. The rear windshield bore a parking decal for the institute. "I'll bet that's De La Rosa. I wonder what he's doing here."

CHAPTER EIGHT

"How do you know him?" Jan asked.

"He did some teaching in Niagara Falls. Tutoring as I recall. He came to a French club meeting once or twice, to spread the word around about his availability."

"Maybe that's what he's doing here. Tutoring that young fellow. Who could be Madame Cartier's son or nephew or something. Maybe that's why she's in Royan."

Gil frowned. "Could be. The only relative I've heard about in connection with her is a granddaughter that no one's seen."

They made their way along the boulevard and another vehicle caught Gil's attention. A grey Peugeot pulled away from the curb and sped off. "Catherine has a car like that," he murmured.

"Surely you don't think it's hers."

"Oh, no. What would she be doing here? She said she had work to do. Lots of grey Peugeots on these streets." Besides, he didn't get a chance to note the license plate and didn't have Catherine's memorized even if he had.

###

Gil no sooner stepped off the elevator and into the hotel's lobby than he spotted Jan and her friends. Liz and Alyssa's fresh tans fairly glowed. "It looks like Royan agrees with you. You ladies look terrific."

Alyssa tossed her pink-and-purple-streaked locks and Liz beamed. "We had a wonderfully relaxing day. After we had our fill of lazing on the beach, we found a bistro for lunch. We had salads again. I never would have thought I'd enjoy salad so much but the food is so fresh and the dressings …" She pinched her thumb and forefinger together and kissed them. "Magnifique!"

"No rabbit this time," Alyssa said. "The waitress suggested another popular dish, a croque monsieur. Like, kind of a ham-and-cheese sandwich kicked up to the next level."

"Apt description," Gil said and chuckled.

"We walked it off window shopping."

"You don't even need store windows to do that," Alyssa said. "The vendors have carts and booths right out on the sidewalk. Paintings and jewelry and crafts and gourmet foods and flowers, everywhere—"

"It's like people live on the sidewalk here. We saw people eating and drinking, playing cards or chess, reading the paper or a magazine, or simply sitting and people-watching. I don't blame them. This weather is perfect for it."

"I love where we live but there are like about two days when you could do that at home."

Liz gave Alyssa a dirty look. "Oh, it's not that bad!"

Alyssa laughed. "Well, you know what I mean."

Through the front door glass, Gil spied Catherine's car pulling into the driveway. "Our ride's here."

Liz and Alyssa linked arms with him. "Let's go."

"Hey, what about me?" Jan cried.

"No worries, girlfriend. He's your guy," Alyssa said. "But for tonight, he's our wingman. You can have him all to yourself as soon as we meet a couple of handsome Royannaises."

Her remark echoed something Jacob had said about Ashley, reminding Gil of tonight's primary mission.

Alyssa and Liz piled into the back seat of Catherine's car. Jan circled to the other door, pausing at the vehicle's rear for a second midway before getting in. Gil took the front passenger seat. The myriad aromas of perfumes and cosmetics permeated the enclosed. Liz and Alyssa chattered about their shopping tour and showed Jan their newly-acquired accessories.

A multicolored glow against the night sky was the first clue they neared the club. The building's façade evoked Monte Carlo's turreted casinos but the teal and salmon paint scheme left no doubt that the facility promised a more carefree experience. A neon-wrapped portico not only created a dramatic entryway, but it also served to funnel arrivals to the front door so entry fees could be collected and identification could be checked.

Catherine got in a queue behind limousines and taxis depositing passengers at the front door.

"We wish you were coming with us," Alyssa said.

"I wish you weren't going at all," Catherine replied. "I still don't like what I've heard about the place."

"We'll keep an eye out for each other," Jan assured her.

Catherine pulled up in front of the entrance. The passengers exited and she shouted, "Call me when you've had all the fun you can stand and I'll come to get you."

"Thanks," said Liz. "We won't keep you up too late."

Gil spotted Jacob and Hope at the portico's entry. "Come on, ladies. Our hosts await. Have your IDs at the ready."

Liz and Alyssa skipped ahead. Jan took Gil's hand.

"Say, what got your attention about Catherine's car back there?" Gil asked. "Do you see something damaged?"

"No, everything was fine. I recalled what you said earlier today and wanted to note the license plate. For future reference."

Gil stopped short. "Future reference for what?"

"I don't know. You're always doing that, scrutinizing license plates, and sometimes that's come in very handy. I'm just trying to help."

"OK," Gil said although Jan's reply failed to mollify his uneasiness.

Jacob and Hope approached the door host first. Admitted, they stood in wait as Gil's party displayed their identification.

"You're all underaged," the door host said.

"We're not and they're with us," Jacob said, pointing to Hope and himself.

The door host frowned. "I don't know. You're barely older than they are."

"But we are old enough," Jacob protested. "They can get in as long as they're in the company of someone who isn't a minor. We've brought friends here before under similar circumstances. I don't understand the problem."

Meanwhile, the crowd forming behind the bottleneck became volubly restless.

"If you'll wait a minute, I want to check with my boss." The door host pulled the velvet rope across the entrance and disappeared into the dark interior. The grumbling behind Gil got louder. A few minutes later the door host returned accompanied by an older man. Beefy with close-cropped hair, he wore a suit with a formidable-looking security badge pinned to the lapel. He asked for Gil and the girls to display their identification cards. Gil had the eeriest sensation that he had seen the man before.

"We just don't want any trouble. You minors, you won't be drinking any alcohol on the premises." The man glowered and said, "You stay together. I don't want to see any of you drifting off by yourself."

"No problem," Hope said.

The man patted the door host on the shoulder. "Good job checking. Let 'em in."

The door host nodded. "Thank you, Mr. Arnaud."

The eerie sensation Gil felt a few minutes ago became an actual chill. He did know the man. George Arnaud worked Security at the store where Gil had been employed. It seemed to Gil then that Arnaud abused his authority, making shoppers surrender their backpacks before entering the store and using his position to move on attractive young women.

And Gil had seen him recently, here in Royan. Arnaud was the man Gil spotted his first day on the beach, the one who chased after a young girl. Gil didn't like it then and he liked it less now.

"Sorry, gang," Jacob said. "We've come here dozens of times and that's never happened before."

"Don't worry about it," Gil said, determined not to let the confrontation ruin the evening.

"Let's see if we can find a table or a place to sit," Jacob hollered over the noise and waded into the crowd.

Gil stepped into the disco and another world. Gone was the soft sea breeze, the sound of the waves, and the peep of shorebirds. The disco was dimly lit, the brightest points being the bar and a spotlight on the DJ. The cacophony of loud music and thousands of conversations flooded his ears, and a mélange of perfumes, aftershaves, and beer filled his nostrils.

They found a free table. Its distance from the DJ and the dance floor made it less sought-after by the rest of the patrons but Gil thought its remote location gave them a modicum of privacy and accommodated a little conversation. The only drawback was its proximity to the swinging doors allowing staff access to the back of the house.

Summer Danger

"They have table service but it can take a while. I'll go to the bar and get drinks for us," Jacob offered.

"I'll go with you and help carry all that back," Gil said. They wove around tables and people toward the bar. Gil had to laugh that table service was a problem. He spied three servers, Mirielle, Celeste, and Collette, but they weren't working, they were dancing, bearing out what Mirielle had told him. The servers did congregate in the same places once they got off work.

He and Jacob elbowed their way to the bar and placed their order. Gil spotted George Arnaud standing off to one side. Arnaud caught his glance and kept Gil and Jacob in view as the bartender supplied their drinks. Arnaud edged over to them and scrutinized their selection.

"All non-alcoholic, I see," he said. He fixed Jacob with a questioning look. "You're old enough to drink."

"I don't need alcohol to have a good time," Jacob replied, "and I didn't want to complicate matters."

Arnaud nodded in approval. "Wise move. Keep it that way and we won't have any problems." He returned to the bar's far side and stepped into the shadow to confer with someone who stood just beyond the light. The figure moved forward and Gil recognized Pierre Desjardins. Desjardins sauntered over and followed Gil and Jacob as they started back to the table.

"I'm glad to see that you in my club," he said to Gil. "Is Catherine with you?"

"No," Gil replied thinking Desjardins may have been one reason she chose to stay away.

People stepped aside to make way for the club's owner enabling Gil and Jacob to move through the crowd.

"We're friends of Ashley Slick," Jacob said.

Dejardins took a puff of his cigarette. "Ashley Slick? I don't know that name."

"You don't? She was an international student who was killed. It was all over the news. This was the last place she was seen alive."

"Is that so? If something had happened here I would certainly know about it."

They reached the table. Gil and Jacob handed out the drinks. Desjardins lingered and Gil felt obligated to make introductions.

"Welcome to the Monte Carlo," Desjardins greeted the teens. "I'm Pierre Dejardins, one of the owners. I hope you enjoy yourselves."

Gil's friends murmured their thanks and assured him they would.

George Arnaud appeared at Dejardins's side. "Pierre, that delivery is here."

Desjardins rolled his eyes. "Sugar. You wouldn't believe the amount of sugar we go through on a nightly basis," he said to Gil and his friends. "Excuse me, duty calls." He and Arnaud left the table and pushed through the swinging doors to the club's backroom.

"So that's the owner," Hope said. "All the times we've been here before we never met him. I was hoping Catherine would come to introduce us."

"Apparently she didn't need to. Looks like Gil and Mr. Desjardins are also acquainted. I guess it's not what you know, it's who you know." Jacob nudged Gil in the ribs.

"I wish he didn't take off right away. I wanted to ask him about Ashley," Hope said.

"I asked him. He denied knowing her," Jacob said.

Hope snorted. "Of course he would deny it. He wouldn't want to be associated with anything like bad publicity for his club."

The conversation halted as they got into their beverages. Alyssa bounced in her seat and wiggled her shoulders in time with the music. Even Gil found himself tapping his foot.

"I didn't think this was what you like to listen to," Jan said.

"Usually it's not but there's catchy something about it."

Liz nodded. "It's called house music and there are particular qualities that make it so popular. It's got an average speed of 120 to 130 beats per minute. Because of the way the brain processes music, it's thought that this rhythm triggers the release of dopamine. That's a 'feel-good' chemical."

"You seem to know a lot about it," Hope said.

Liz smiled. "I researched it for a guest blog post I wrote."

"120, 130, I don't care how many beats there are. I want to dance to all of them. Who's ready to get out on the floor?" Alyssa slid off her stool.

Liz laughed. "OK, Dancing Queen, let's see if we can't burn off some of your nervous energy."

"Come on, Jacob. Let's go," Hope said. "Gil? Jan?"

"I'd rather wait for a slow dance," Gil replied. "There will be a slow dance, won't there?"

"Yeah, there will. OK, you hold down the table then."

The four dived into the crowd.

"I hope that was OK with you," Gil said to Jan.

"Fine. I'm not complaining about having you all to myself."

Gil leaned over to kiss her cheek. Straightening, his attention was snared by a sight across the room. "I can't believe it."

"What?" Jan asked, patting her face. "Is my makeup out of place?"

"No, no. Nothing wrong with how you look," he replied. He smiled and said, "You look fantastic. No, it's over there, at the bar. Talking to Pierre. Those two women."

Jan scowled. "If I look so good, why are you eyeing other women?"

"They're the two German women I met on the beach the first day I was here. The ones who said they knew Catherine but she denied it. And then I saw them later, much later. I was jet-lagged. I couldn't sleep. I went for a late-night walk on the beach and saw them there. Talking with—yes, I'm certain of it now—with Pierre Desjardins. I knew when I met him the next day that I'd seen him before. What were they doing on the beach at that hour?"

"Well, buddy, you were there and there wasn't anything suspicious about that."

"And what are they doing here now, with him?"

"It's a public place. Maybe they came to dance. And if they know him, which it seems they do …"

"Hmm. I guess you're right. Well, where was I?"

"I believe you were about to kiss me."

"So I was," Gil said and followed through on his original impulse.

"Thanks for a lovely day," she said. "I know you had ulterior motives and were secretly sleuthing—"

"Not so secretly, since you figured that out."

"Still, I enjoyed the sights."

Looking over Jan's shoulder, Gil's gaze found another familiar face. "Speaking of today's sleuthing, you won't believe who's here. It's Madame Cartier."

"Where?"

"At the end of the bar. It looks like she's talking to Desjardins. What's she doing at a disco?"

"You did say she keeps trying to match her granddaughter up with some guy. Plenty of single guys here, that's for sure."

"But talking to Desjardins? What does she want with him?" Gil snorted. "She can't be trying to entice him to meet her mythical granddaughter. If she exists at all."

"Maybe the woman is hoping he'll introduce her to a likely candidate."

"That's what I love about you, Jan. You're always ready to give people the benefit of the doubt."

"And you're always on guard. No one's ever going to take you by surprise."

"But I get the feeling you have doubts about Catherine."

"I dunno. She seems to know an awful lot about drugs."

"She explained that. She's surrounded by it. There's a lot of drug abuse in the entertainment industry." He frowned. "You're not implying …?"

"I'm not implying anything. But how much do you know about her?"

"Jan, she's my cousin. We've corresponded regularly for years."

"'Corresponded.' That's my point. Letters, emails, texts, social media. It's all virtual. It's been some time since you've been with her. You don't see her every day. As far as what she does, you know only what she tells you."

"I can't believe what you're saying!"

"I'm not saying anything. Look, forget it. She and I are hardly acquainted. I need to get to know her better. And I'd like to since you're so fond of her." She took both Gil's hands in hers. "I certainly don't want to fight about it. I'd rather enjoy being with you."

"I'm sorry. It's that Desjardins. The man bugs me. There's something sub rosa about that guy."

"Try to put it out of your mind. Come on, let's dance. They're playing our song."

"They are? What is it?" Not only did Gil not recall the tune being among his favorites, but he also didn't recognize it at all. Its beat was appealing enough but it had no words. It sounded so electronic he couldn't identify what instruments were being used. "We have a song?"

"We do now," Jan said and tugged him toward the dance floor.

CHAPTER NINE

Gil and Jan joined the throng of people gyrating on the dance floor.

"If this is our song, what's the name of it?" Gil asked.

Jan laughed. "I have no idea. If we get a chance I'll ask the DJ or someone."

Gil frowned. "Then what makes it our song?"

"It is the one that was playing the night we almost argued but didn't."

Gil leaned close and kissed her on the lips. The pounding beat shifted into something like a languid heartbeat accompanied by dreamy words vocalized by Taylor Swift, a singer even Gil recognized. Gil pulled

Jan into an embrace. "Now this is more like it," he whispered in her ear.

"Mmm." She pressed against him and rested her head against his shoulder.

The congestion eased as some dancers conceded the floor to couples. Gil became spellbound by the aroma of Jan's perfume and the warmth of her closeness. Through half-closed eyes, he guided them in a tight circle then stopped.

Jan raised her head. "What?"

"That man, talking with Desjardins. I think that's De la Rosa. I saw him today at Madame Cartier's house and now he's here."

Taking the lead, Jan got Gil moving to the music again. "Is that unusual?"

"I guess not. Jacob said he's seen the man here before. But he also said Ashley was talking with him that night."

"You want to ask him about it, don't you?"

Gil did but fought the urge. The strange occurrences that unnerved him had tarnished enough of Jan's visit. Desjardin, Arnaud, the German women, Madame Cartier, and now De la Rosa, all in the same establishment at the same time. Jan's explanations of why they were at the Monte Carlo all made sense but didn't ease his anxiety. Seeing them with their heads together would be the last straw.

The song ended and Gil led them to their table. Jacob had ordered a second round.

"What do I owe you?" Gil asked.

"Nothing. I owe you for the lunch at La Fiesta and breakfast at the Doux Secret."

Catherine had picked up those tabs but Gil didn't argue. "Hey, where's Alyssa?"

Liz patted her face. "Went to powder her nose." She sipped her drink. "Of course, you all know that's a euphemism for 'she had to pee' but did you know how that came about? At one time, women used face powder instead of liquid makeup. Ladies' rooms had chairs and counters and mirrors so women could retouch their makeup. But going even further back, a powder room was where you went to refresh the powder in your wig."

Her recitation earned a moment of stunned silence from her audience.

Jacob ran the back of his hand across his forehead. "Phew. Am I relieved I won't have to go through the rest of my life not knowing that."

Jan asked, "You know this because—"

"You wrote a guest blog post about it?" Hope asked.

Liz grinned and nodded.

"Did you know Mr. De la Rosa's here?" Gil asked Jacob.

Jacob sipped his drink. "Yeah, I saw him. Funny you should mention him. He was talking with your friend Alyssa. Maybe he convinced her to come to the institute. We'd take good care of her, wouldn't we, Hope?"

"Mr. Leduc."

Gil turned his head toward the voice. "Mr. Beaumer."

Jacob sat taller in his seat while Hope cringed.

"I'm surprised to see you here, Mr. Leduc. I thought you'd received sufficient warning to stay away."

Jacob planted his palms on the tabletop. "This is where our friend was last seen. We wanted to see if we could learn anything."

Beaumer's eyebrows rose. "And have you?"

"Well, not yet." He jutted out his chin. "We were going to question the owner, Pierre Desjardins but he got called away. Something about a delivery."

Beaumer remarked, "We've already had a conversation with Mr. Desjardins."

"And what did he tell you?" Gil asked.

Beaumer gave him an indulgent smile.

"You wouldn't tell us if he did, would you?" Hope said.

"You know, Mr. De la Rosa is here," Jacob said. "The tutor from the institute. We told you he was here the same night Ashley was. We saw them talking."

"We've had a conversation with Mr. De la Rosa," Beaumer replied.

"You know who else is here?" Gil asked. "That Madame Cartier. The woman who badgered me on the train from Paris."

"Has she badgered you since?"

"No. But she's up to something. I've seen her everywhere. At the institute, at church. OK, I didn't see her at church myself but a member told me that she's persona non grata there. I saw her this morning, at her house, with De la Rosa."

"You saw her at her home." Beaumer glared. "What were you doing there? Are you stalking her?"

Jan sprang from her seat. "Gil doesn't stalk people."

"And you know who else is here tonight? George Arnaud."

"Or course Arnaud is here," Beaumer replied. "He's the bouncer. Excuse me; he works 'Security.' Have you already had a run-in with him?"

"We have not!" Hope said.

"And why are you here tonight?" Gil asked. "Is there trouble?"

"Not so far. Let's keep it that way. It would be best if you gave this place a wide berth." Beaumer turned on his heels and left without asking about Catherine, in whom he'd been so interested before.

Summer Danger

Hope said, "Jacob, I'd like to leave. I don't want to stay if he's going to be eyeballing us all night like we're suspects."

"What do you say, Gil? Time to go?"

Gil looked at Liz and Jan who nodded their agreement. "I'll call Catherine. And where's Alyssa?"

Liz slid off her stool. "I'll go check the ladies' room. Meet you out front?"

"Sounds good."

Gil dialed Catherine. Unlike the other night, she answered at the first ring. 'I'll be right there."

They bid Jacob and Hope goodbye. They no sooner reached the door than they saw Catherine's car idling in the driveway.

"How'd you get here so fast?" Jan asked.

"You haven't been parked here all night waiting for us?" Gil said.

Catherine laughed. "Hardly. It's just easier at this hour than when everyone's trying to get in." She popped open all the door locks. "Say, where's the other two, Liz and Alyssa?"

"Here they are."

Gripping Alyssa's arm, Liz had her literally in tow. Waving her other arm, skipping, and singing, Alyssa didn't appear at all ready to leave.

"Are you OK?" Gil asked.

"I've never been so OK in my whole life," Alyssa cried. "Whoop whoop whoop!"

Jim Toner

They bundled into Catherine's car and she pulled away. They'd traveled barely five miles when Alyssa's giddy laughter became a groan. "Oh, maybe I don't feel so OK anymore. I'm queasy."

"Alyssa? Say, does anyone have a bottle of water or something? I think she's choking."

The groaning became gasping.

"My chest hurts. I can't breathe."

"Alyssa!" Liz cried.

"Gil, do you have a hanky?" Jan asked. "Alyssa's got a nosebleed."

Catherine slowed and glanced into the back seat. "Oh, no," she said. She turned off the boulevard onto a side street and parked against the curb. She switched on the overhead light and twisted in her seat. "Oh, no. Nik Nak," she breathed. She whipped back to the steering wheel and the car lurched from the curb. Weaving into traffic, she said, "We're not going to the hotel. We're going to the hospital."

"The hospital?" Gil replied. "Do you think she's that ill? What—"

"I do," Catherine said. Hunched over the steering wheel she muttered what sounded to Gil like "Drug overdose."

"Should we call an ambulance?"

"By the time they reach us, I will have gotten her there." Catherine punched the car's hazard-flashers button and pulled the light stalk to pulse the headlights. "But you can call the hospital and alert them we're on our way. Tell them to have a crash cart ready."

"Crash cart! Do you think she's having a heart attack?" Liz asked. "What can we do?"

"See my handbag? I've got a cosmetics bag in it. You'll find a travel-size bottle of aspirin. Give her one," Catherine replied. "Not the other painkillers, the aspirin. Gil, did you get through to the hospital?"

"Yes. They'll be ready for us."

"Do you have Francois Beaumer's number?"

"He's got mine, that's for sure. He gave me his card. It's in my room—"

"Never mind. Take my phone. It's in my Contacts." She waved at the console.

Gil scrolled through the "B" listings. "It's not here."

"Under 'F'," Catherine said. She jerked the wheel to swerve around a car. "Get him on the phone."

Catherine was on a first-name basis with the police officer? Gil pressed the "Call" symbol. He expected the police department switchboard to answer and was startled when Beaumer picked up.

"It's Gil Leduc. I'm with Catherine Robert. We're headed for the hospital. She wanted you to know—"

"Put him on speaker," Catherine said. "Francois, it's one of Gil's friends. I think it's an overdose. She must have gotten it at the club. She was fine a few hours ago when I dropped them off."

Beaumer made a growling noise. "Just what I was there to prevent. I'll meet you at the hospital. Don't break any traffic laws getting there." He ended the call.

Catherine snorted and the car leaped forward. She cut around other vehicles sometimes using the shoulder. With not a single wrong turn or hesitation she bulled her way through traffic, drawing honking horns and screeching tires from motorists who didn't get out of her way fast enough. She pulled under the hospital's Emergency Room portico and screeched to a stop. Scrub-suited personnel stood at the entrance. Catherine flung open the car door, stepped out, and waved to them. They trundled a gurney over. "She's in the back seat," Catherine said.

Members of the ER team hoisted Alyssa onto the gurney and whisked her into the hospital. Another approached Catherine. "Admitting is going to need some information. Would you come with me?"

"Come on, everybody," Catherine said. "You'll have better answers than I will."

A frantic hour later, Liz and Jan had gotten Alyssa officially admitted. They along with Catherine and Gil were steered to a quiet lounge away from the ER lobby's clamor where they joined other patients' concerned friends and family to await news. A volunteer told them coffee and tea were available but they were all too tense.

At last, the volunteer called them over to her station. "I've got information from the ER team. Your friend has been stabilized. Good work on getting her here so quickly. And I'm told the aspirin helped to minimize the damage. We've got a long road ahead and a lot of work to do but she's out of immediate danger."

Gil and friends all took deep breaths. Jan and Liz collapsed into armchairs. "Would anyone like coffee?" Gil asked. Jan and Liz raised limp hands. Catherine joined Gil at the console table.

Gil filled foam cups from an urn. He handed one to Catherine. "Where did you learn to drive like that?" Gil asked. "I mean, I've seen you do it on the show."

Catherine dismissed that with a wave. "That's not me. That's a stunt driver dubbed in. But I did take a defensive driving course so I could give a realistic portrayal."

"And you knew the exact location of the hospital. All the shortcuts and where the traffic lights are."

Catherine was about to respond when Francois Beaumer burst into the room and strode across to join them.

CHAPTER TEN

Beaumer scowled at Gil. "Were you not told to stay away from that place?"

"I was there to find out what happened to my friend," Gil replied, trying not to sound defensive. He stepped closer to Beaumer, narrowing the gap between them. "Now another friend has been hurt. Isn't it your job to stop this?"

"It is," Beaumer replied, his face flushed. "I was chasing down a lead."

That gave Gil pause. "What lead?"

"Desjardins got a late-night delivery."

"He mentioned something about that."

"I didn't like the sound of it. I followed the truck to see what I could learn. Unfortunately, the driver gave me no reason to pull him over. I planned to trail him to his next stop when you and Catherine called about your friend. Now, why don't you tell me, minute by minute, what she was up to in the club?"

Gil did, to the point when he and Jan returned from the dance floor to learn that Alyssa went to the ladies' room. "It seemed to me she was there a long time. I didn't give it much thought. Sometimes there are lines of women waiting to get into the restroom, especially at sporting events at halftime."

"Go on."

"Jacob told me that she had been talking with De la Rosa. He said the same about Ashley, the last time anyone saw her. Coincidence?"

"I don't like coincidences. I'll follow up with De la Rosa. But you, you leave this to me." Beaumer jabbed the air in front of Gil's face with his index finger. "I don't want you making any of these characters so nervous they clam up or leave town."

It wasn't a promise Gil wanted to make. He gave Beaumer a grunt he trusted the man would take as an assent.

"I hope your friend will be OK. Keep me posted."

"Maybe you can do me the same courtesy," Gil said. "We don't even know how Ashley died."

Beaumer chewed his lip. "I suppose I can tell you. It will be made public soon enough. Heart attack."

"Ashley? But she was my age."

With a shrug, Beaumer turned and buttonholed Catherine. "And you, young lady, I understand you ran 'red-lights-and-sirens' getting here."

Catherine pouted. "I ran not one single red light."

The doctor appeared in the lounge and summoned Alyssa's friends to gather around. "Your friend is out of immediate danger but I'm afraid not out of the woods," she said. "She had a heart attack."

Liz looked pale, Jan and Catherine grim.

"A heart attack?" Gil said. "Same as Ashley. Beaumer just told me."

"So Ashley wasn't injured in a traffic accident," Jan said.

"Nor was she assaulted." Liz bit her lip and shuddered.

"But Alyssa's so young. How can that be?"

"That's often a reaction to cocaine—"

"Cocaine?" Liz gaped.

"It's a stimulant drug. It excites the central nervous system, increases the heart rate, and raises blood pressure," the doctor said. "Of course, for someone her age and apparent level of fitness—"

"She's an athlete," Liz blurted. "She, Jan, and I play softball."

The doctor nodded. "That's worked to her advantage. We saw no other signs of cardiac issues. We determined it was a response to the drug—"

"Alyssa doesn't use drugs," Liz protested.

The doctor gave her a patient smile. "We also didn't find immediate signs of chronic drug abuse. This could indeed have been an infrequent—or even first time—occurrence. It's a shock to the body. We've got her heart rhythm stabilized but she took in more than simply cocaine. We're working to counter the effects of those other chemicals." She shook her head and muttered. "We're seeing too many of these, and recently. Someone needs to get this NikNak off the streets." She grimaced, said "If you'll excuse me," and hurried away.

"NikNak," Jan echoed. "Didn't Beaumer mention that when he looked at Ashley?" She narrowed her eyes at Catherine. "And you said the same thing tonight about Alyssa." Her grim expression demanded a response.

"It's an amped-up form of cocaine. It's almost immediately addictive which is why the dealers love it so much. It creates instant customers."

"If they don't die first," Liz grumbled.

"As if it's not dangerous enough by itself, it's often cut with deadly adulterants. It's inhaled and often ruptures blood vessels in the nose, so victims have telltale pink froth around their nostrils."

"Like Alyssa," Liz said.

Catherine nodded.

"And Ashley," Gil added.

"You saw that?" Jan asked.

"I saw something, a discoloration around her nose. I didn't know exactly what I was seeing at the time but that sounds about right."

Jan frowned. "Why do you know so much about this, Catherine?"

"I told you."

"Yes. You said there's a lot of abuse in the entertainment industry. But there's more to it, isn't there? Have you tried it?"

Catherine recoiled. "Me? No." She sighed. "But there was a gal on the set, a young actress. It was her first important role. Her character didn't even have a name, just 'Shop Cashier,' but she had some lines. It got her name in the credits. That's a huge step up. She was so nervous about it, about making the most out of it she possibly could. That's why she tried cocaine. Someone told her it would bolster her confidence." Catherine shook her head. "Instead it killed her."

Liz's shoulders slumped and Jan looked drawn.

"There isn't any more we can do here," Catherine said. "Let's go back to the hotel. The hospital has our contact information. They'll let us know if there are any developments."

The girls nodded. Arms draped across each other's shoulders, they trudged to the exit.

Gil walked alongside Catherine.

"Now I know what's behind it. I want to know who's behind it. Who's putting this stuff on the street, putting it in the hands of people who don't know what they're getting into?"

Catherine stopped short. "No, you don't, Gil. This is dangerous stuff, dangerous people. Lots of money is at stake and they will stop at nothing to stay in the game. Leave this to the police."

"People keep telling me that but I don't see them doing anything. De la Rosa's got to be involved. Desjardins, too; the Monte Carlo was connected with both Ashley and Alyssa. Beaumer said he 'had a conversation' with both men but what did that accomplish? I want to start with De la Rosa. His name keeps coming up. He's been at the scene too many times. I'd like to have a chat with him."

"And what are you going to say?"

"I'll ask him. Directly. About Ashley. Alyssa too. I can ask him questions the police can't. Their hands are tied by regulations and procedures."

Catherine clasped his shoulders. "Don't. Just don't."

Gil grunted. As he had with Beaumer, he hoped Catherine would take his nonverbal reply as an assent.

Catherine piloted the Peugeot toward the Hôtel Bord du Mer at a much more respectable speed than what propelled them to the hospital.

The next morning, though Gil rose later than usual, the extra hours of sleep didn't leave him alert and refreshed. Instead, he woke feeling dazed and out of sorts, the way a nightmare sometimes affected him. He called Jan only to learn that everyone else was up and already at breakfast. He raced through dressing and hurried to join them.

He found them nursing cups of coffee and glasses of juice. Lavishly-laden plates sat before them, barely picked at. Glum expressions and shadowed eyes told him that no one slept well.

No sooner had he sat then Celeste brought him his "usual" hot chocolate but not even the sweet beverage could brighten his mood. When Celeste remarked, "Look at you, here with your harem," all he could do was respond with a grumble.

"I'm thinking of calling Jacob," he told his tablemates. "He and Hope should know about what happened and I don't want them to learn about it from the media."

"If they haven't already," Jan said with a sour expression.

Gil fired up his mobile. Jacob answered almost immediately "Hey, Gil, I'm headed for class. Can I call you back?"

"Sure. I was thinking of coming by. I have some news to share. Would you have time today?"

"I've got a break at noon. How about we meet on the beach at Le Grande Conche? There's a brasserie right on the strand. I can grab lunch."

"You're on. If Hope is free, bring her along."

"Gotta go," Jacob said and rang off.

Gil set the phone down. "Meeting Jacob and Hope at noon. What's everyone else got planned?"

Liz said, "I'd like to go back to the hospital and check on Alyssa, bring her fresh clothes and toiletries she might want when she's up and about. They might even let me see her. I know I'm not immediate family but I'm as close as she'll get here."

"Catherine?"

"I've got a conference call with the show's PR agency to go over the campaign for the new season."

"Here you are at this fabulous beach resort and you have to work?"

Catherine gave Liz a pained smile. "At least I can sit outside in the sun while I'm on the phone." She offered to give Liz a ride to the hospital before her meeting.

Gil and Jan meandered in the opposite direction to meet up with Jacob. Jan spotted a sign for a florist and suggested they send flowers to Alyssa. Hoping to cheer Jan, Gil bought her a nosegay wrist bouquet.

"Aren't you sweet?" she said, inhaling the flowers' fragrance.

At a souvenir shop, she bought tee shirts for friends back home. "Yeah, tee shirts. I know, it's tacky and corny. But they pack so well and won't put my luggage overweight and one size usually fits all—"

Gil held up his hand. "You won't get any argument from me."

They wandered through the marina where hundreds of boats docked, small open fishing boats alongside luxury yachts. They chuckled at the clever names with which owners had christened their vessels.

"What do you suppose they were thinking?" Jan asked, pointed to one named Loose Shadow. She chuckled at Fishy Prospect. "I'll bet the owners are new to boating. Oh, that's cute," she said of You and Me Boat.

They passed one labeled High Hopes. "That one sounds like a drug runner," Gil said.

"You don't think someone would be that obvious, do you?"

They made their way back to the roadway between the docks and the parking lot. Sandwiched between two less ostentatious vehicles, a red Citroen stood out. "I think that's Pierre Desjardins's car," Gil said.

"Really?"

"I saw him pull away in one just like that the night we were at the church."

"Are you sure it's the same one?"

"I only caught part of the license plate number but I'd bet on it. What would it be doing here?" Gil craned his neck to get a closer look. The vehicle was unoccupied.

"He probably pulls in good money from the club. It's not unreasonable to think he would own a boat and he's taking a work break."

"No, I guess not."

They continued walking. "Gil, look. Isn't that Catherine's car?" Jan pointed to a grey Peugeot.

"In the marina parking lot? Why would it be here?"

Jan's eyes narrowed. "As long as we're taking bets, I'm placing mine on it. I did check the license plate and I'd swear that's her car."

"Can't be. She's taking Liz to the hospital. And that's in the other direction."

"If you say so," Jan replied and Gil didn't belabor the point but the thought made him uneasy. Desjardins and Catherine both in the marina at the same time? Together?

CHAPTER ELEVEN

Gil pictured his cousin and the club owner lounging on the deck of one of the moored boats, enjoying cocktails and the sunshine. Catherine had denied a relationship with Desjardin yet here was evidence that suggested the contrary. Gil kept his misgivings to himself but determined to quiz his cousin about it later.

He and Jan found the brasserie easily enough. A low white building with a bold sign, it boasted an abundance of seating on its outdoor deck. Part brewery, part cafeteria, the brasserie did a booming lunchtime business. Gil and Jan wove around crowded tables before finding Jacob and Hope.

Jacob apologized for having ordered already. "We've got to get back to class."

Gil assured him it wasn't a problem. "We know you're not on vacation."

He and Jan perused the menus with offered everything from casual eats to full meals but the view captured Jan's attention. "What's that?" she asked, pointed out across the water.

"Oh, that. That's the Cordouan Lighthouse."

"Wow, a lighthouse! Is it still in operation? I wonder if visitors can go there," she said.

"They can," said the waitress as she set down Jan and Gil's drinks. "We are very proud of Le Phare. It is a historic monument, just like the Notre Dame in Paris. It's the oldest French lighthouse still in operation. The waters where the Gironde meets the Atlantic are very turbulent so a lighthouse is a boon to sailors. Le Phare was built in 1360—it was a much more humble structure then. When it was rebuilt it was made 'fit for a King.' The interior is gorgeous and the view from the top, stunning—if you can manage climbing over 300 steps," she said with a grin. "You really must go see. If you have a boat, you can buy an admission ticket from the lighthouse keepers—"

"Keepers?" Hope said. "People live there?"

"They do."

"Oh, I would love to live in a lighthouse, wouldn't you?" she asked her friends.

"What if you don't have a boat?" Gil wanted to know.

"You can book a visit that includes a boat crossing." the waitress replied. "Well, I've kept you waiting long enough. I'll go put in your orders."

"She was a font of knowledge," Jacob said.

"The servers usually are." It was Celeste who first mentioned the Monte Carlo to him. Gil now wondered why she didn't say anything about its sullied reputation when that was well-known to Catherine, an out-of-towner.

"A famous lighthouse right here in Royan. I learned something new." Jacob took a swallow of beer. "You said you had news. Did you find out more about the investigation into Ashley's death?"

"I wish. No, this is something else although it could be related." Gil told Jacob and Hope what happened to Alyssa after they parted at the club.

Hope's hand when to her mouth and her face paled. "No," she breathed.

Jacob planted his palms on the table. "But she was fine last night. She was having a blast. What happened?" He shook his head. "It's not like she had too much to drink. We were all drinking soft drinks, the better to keep that bouncer off our backs."

"That's what I'd like to know," Gil replied.

"You said it was related to Ashley," Hope said.

"We learned Ashley had a heart attack, brought about by cocaine."

Hope scoffed. "No way. Ashley didn't do drugs."

"Neither did Alyssa," Jan said. "That they didn't may have been a contributing factor. It was such a shock to their bodies. Plus, this is an especially strong form of cocaine. Or so Catherine says."

Feeling oddly defensive of his cousin, Gil reminded her, "The doctor said the same thing." He pushed the food around on his plate. "And here's another thing they had in common: Mr. De la Rosa."

"How's that?" Jacob asked.

"They both encountered him at the club."

Jacob frowned. "Are you saying Mr. De la Rosa gave them cocaine? That he's dealing?"

"Is that so unbelievable? He's in a perfect place for it. Surrounded by young people, some of them impressionable, far from home, maybe for the first time. Alone in a foreign country, away from family and friends. Trying to fit in. And here he is, an authority figure who's friendly and sociable. He could easily gain their trust."

Hope bit her lower lip. "I hate thinking an instructor could exploit his position that way."

Jacob stroked his chin. "Say, I see a couple of kids over there; I think they're students at the institute. Maybe they know more about him than we do. I'll go ask."

From where Gil sat he couldn't hear the conversation. But the other students smiled, waved Jacob an invitation to sit, regarded him with attention, and nodded.

Jacob returned to Gil and friends and retook his seat. "I don't know what to think now," he said. "They don't have any classes with him but they do know who he is. They also more or less know who Ashley was, or at least heard that a student went missing. I told them what happened and they weren't surprised. It's rumored that if you want chemical assistance with your studies, he's the man to see."

"Rumor," Gil grumbled. "We don't need rumors, we need facts."

"That's not even true," Hope said. "About cocaine, that is. It doesn't at all help you concentrate, focus, remember—"

"I guess truth in advertising is not a hallmark of the drug trade," Jacob replied. "Anyway, no one ever mentioned that to me."

"You hang with the wrong crowd," Jan said.

"Or the right one." Jacob polished off his lunch and drained his beer. "Speaking of studies, we should be heading back. Keep us posted about Alyssa, OK?"

Gil promised he would. He picked at his lunch but had no appetite.

"Oh, I know that look," Jan said. "You're frustrated."

"It's all questions and no answers."

Jan got out her phone. "I'll check in with Liz. Maybe Alyssa's come around and can tell us what happened." Liz apparently answered promptly but Jan's forehead became furrowed with worry lines. Her side of the conversation was mostly "uh-huh" and "OK." She set the phone down. "Alyssa's still in intensive care. They wouldn't let Liz see her. They won't let anyone see her, not even the police."

"So we won't be getting confirmation from her about De la Rosa."

Jan shook her head. "Catherine took Liz back to the hotel. Liz said she would go down to the pool, try to distract herself with some reading or writing. So, what next, Buddy?"

"I'd like to follow Jacob and Hope back to the institute, find De la Rosa, and hold his feet to the fire."

"I know you would. But the school is his turf. He's likely to get you thrown out for trespassing or harassment or something."

Gil held his hands up in surrender. "As usual, you are right. What would you suggest?"

Jan narrowed her eyes. "Why don't we go do that?" She pointed towards the Conche de Foncillon.

"What? That?"

"Could we? Could we please?" Jan's eyes shone and she bounced in her chair.

"You nut! Sure, if you want to."

"Why not? It might help take our minds off all this upsetting stuff."

"You're on. Let's head that way. We can cut across the beach."

"Now you're talking."

They had gone a few blocks when Gil said, "Could you wait a second? I want to make one little detour. I, uh, want to ask if they have a restroom."

Jan gave him a stern look. "You couldn't go before we left the brasserie?"

Gil shrugged. "I'll just be a minute." He ducked into the Tourist Office. When he rejoined Jan he said, "I would hate to be sorry I didn't make that stop when I had the chance."

They continued across the sand and around the marina. Jan said nothing about spotting Catherine's Peugeot and Gil didn't mention Desjardins's Citroen but the silence as they passed between the cars and the boats left Gil thinking about the argument they almost had about Catherine in the club.

Jan perked up at the sight of their destination. She kissed Gil on the cheek. "Thanks for agreeing to this."

"There's a line. You're sure you want to wait?"

"It'll be worth it."

Gil hoped so. Ahead and behind them, children pitched fits about the delay.

Inching forward, Jan reminisced about the places she and her friends had been in England. "I do hope Alyssa will recover."

"Sounds like you had a great time," Gil said. "I'm sorry about everything that's gone on since you here."

Jan hugged him. "None of that's your fault. And it doesn't change the fact that I'm happy to be here with you. Look, it's our turn."

"As if we haven't been going around in circles for days now."

"Gil!" Jan bopped his arm. "Put all that away, just for a few minutes, will you?"

"OK." Gil stepped up to the ticket booth. "Two, please."

The clerk exchanged ticket stubs for the entry fee. "Enjoy Le Gran Roue."

"The Gran Roue," Jan echoed.

"That means the Big Wheel."

"And it is big. But it sounds so much cooler in French. There's one in London on the Thames. It's called the Eye. We didn't have time to go. I wonder why we call them Ferris wheels."

"I'll bet Liz knows. She's probably written a guest blog post about it."

Jan laughed and mounted the carriage. Gil got in beside her and they fastened their safety belts.

"It's like sitting in an oversized teacup," Jan said. "I feel like Alice in Wonderland."

The wheel made its languid climb to the tune of laughter and squeals from children in the other carriages.

"Gil, this is fabulous. What a view!" Jan stretched to the left and the right. "I can see the whole city and the beaches and estuary. Royan is a beautiful place. I'm so glad I got a chance to come and enjoy it with you."

Gil smiled. His head in the clouds, he felt lifted away from mysterious deaths, unanswered questions, and nagging suspicions. He leaned over and kissed Jan. "This was a good idea. You were right. Again."

The wheel made another revolution. At the apex, Jan plucked petals from her corsage and tossed them into the wind. "For Ashley," she said. "And for Alyssa. May God bless them both." The petals caught a thermal and they hung in space. Like the enigmas surrounding their tragedies, Gil thought, as the wheel brought them back to Earth.

They returned to the hotel and found Liz stretched out on a lounge chair by the pool. She laid her book in her lap.

"Have you been here by yourself all day?" Jan asked.

"Not all day. Catherine picked me up from the hospital, brought me back then said she had some errands to run."

Gil wondered if those errands included a rendezvous with Pierre Desjardins on his boat.

Jan settled on a nearby chair. "It was rude of us to desert you and leave you alone."

"Nonsense," Liz said, "A book lover is never alone." She lifted the book from her lap and waved it. "Anyway, I haven't been here all day. I took myself for thalassotherapy."

"Thalass—what's that?" Gil asked.

"Seawater treatments. France is noted for its thalassotherapy and Royan is a major thalassotherapy center. The treatments closer to the English channel are invigorating while the ones closer to the Mediterranean are soothing. The thalassotherapy here is tonic, cleansing. It's recommended for dealing with stress, burnout, exhaustion—sound familiar?"

Jan nodded.

"I had a jet treatment where I was sprayed with seawater at a therapeutic temperature and pressure, to drive out toxins and tension, and a mud mask on my face." She patted her cheek. "Don't I look refreshed?"

"You do," Jan said.

"I feel better too. Like the therapy washed away some of the strain of the last two days."

"Wouldn't a dunk in the Gironde accomplish the same thing?" Gil asked.

Jan and Liz scowled. Liz said, "It's recommended that one have a series of treatments over days and weeks. I won't be here long enough but I had a little hint of what it could do. I bought a travel set with different preparations—mud packs and seaweed bath soak and marine cream—we can use them at home."

Jan told her about the therapy to which she and Gil had treated themselves. Liz thought that sounded just as beneficial as a seaweed bath.

"Any word about Alyssa?" Gil asked.

Liz shook her head. "I called a while ago. She's still in intensive care. The flowers you sent arrived. The nurses don't want to put them in an ICU room but they'll keep them watered and nice for her when she's moved to less critical care. The good news is that possibly tomorrow she can have visitors. Just a few at a time and for a short while only. We can call in the morning and get an update."

"Visitors, huh? I hope the cops don't muscle in and wear her out." Jan said.

"I wonder if they've learned anything new about Ashley." Gil wished that like Catherine he had Francois Beaumer's direct line. He called the station but couldn't get any further than the general receptionist. "We'll forward your inquiry to the investigating officer," he was told. "You'll be contacted if there's information."

"Speaking of wear, I don't know about the two of you but I'm thinking of an early night. Something to eat and then read myself to sleep. I'd like to stay in the zone that the thalassotherapy put me in," Liz said.

Jan agreed. "I've had enough of clubbing for a while. How about you, Gil?"

Gil had to admit he was fatigued. He had a mild headache from trying to make all the pieces fit.

They agreed to freshen up and meet in the hotel restaurant for a light dinner. Gil called Catherine to ask if she cared to join them. She begged off saying she had plans to get together with a friend. Gil wasn't aware that his cousin knew anyone in Royan to socialize with and almost asked, "Pierre Desjardins?"

The three friends passed up entrees and dined on salads and slices of cold meat, fish, and vegetable terrines. For dessert, they passed around verrines. The small clear glass dishes displayed contrasting layers of fruit, custard cream, and streusel. Weary, downhearted spirits showed in the lackluster conversation. Rather than linger in the restaurant they bid each other goodnight and retired early.

As worn out as he was, Gil couldn't fall asleep. Jet-lag his first night in Royan affected him the same way. A late-night stroll helped him unwind then and might work again. He stepped out of the hotel intending to walk on the beach. Instead, his feet took him to through the parking lot and the route he and Jan took.

He gave the cars a passing glance hoping that Catherine's car would be there, that she wasn't still out with Pierre—correction, her "friend." He spotted her Peugeot at the back of the lot just out of the corona of illumination from the floodlight on the hotel's rear wall. Gil hated himself for what he was about to do. He loved his cousin but he loved and trusted Jan, too. Though he didn't for a minute share her doubts about Catherine, he continued to cross the lot.

I'll memorize the license plate, he told himself. Then someday the opportunity will present itself to compare notes with Jan. She'll be proved wrong and that would put his mind at ease.

He neared the car. The passenger compartment was dark. Good, he thought. He'd hate to run into Catherine and her "friend" and have to explain why he was cruising the hotel parking lot late at night. He circled to the car's rear and saw the trunk lid was ajar. That wouldn't be safe. Anyone could access the vehicle and steal it. Gil reached out to lower the lid but it got hung up. Something was blocking it. He stepped forward to push the obstacle farther back and stopped.

It wasn't a package. It was a body.

CHAPTER TWELVE

Gil staggered backward, his breath lodged in his throat, his pulse pounding in his ears.

A body. In Catherine's car. It was outrageous, incredible.

From where he stood he could make out a pair of trousered legs and Oxford-ed feet. A man's body, most likely. Was it Desjardins? Did he threaten Catherine and did she …?

No, that was ridiculous, Gil decided. Even if she resorted to extreme measures to protect herself, why would she leave the body in her car?

He could drag the body out and shove it under some bushes, make it look like the dead man was a victim of random violence. Gil nixed that idea as soon as it popped into his head. There would still be plenty of incriminating forensic evidence left in the vehicle.

He needed to call her but damn, he left his phone in his room. He would have to go back inside. Then what? Call Catherine and ask her what she knew about it? Forget he saw anything, return to his room, and let someone else make the grisly discovery? But what if he'd been seen? The night clerk might have observed him leaving, might have noticed the time. Sooner later, investigators would discover Gil had been near the car. They'd want to know what he was doing there and why he left without notifying anyone.

There was no help for it. He'd have to report it. Gil trudged back to the lobby. The only question was whom to call first, the cops or Catherine?

As when he found Ashley's body outside the Hôtel Les Bleuets, a short-sleeved officer left his beach patrol to respond to the call. Gil and Catherine led the man to the parking lot.

"Don't I know you?" the policeman asked Gil. "Yes, you found the body outside the Hôtel Les Bleuets two days ago." The policeman glowered. "Do you make a habit of this?"

Gil chose not to dignify the question with an answer.

"Never mind. I'll get police judiciare on the scene." The officer reached for his radio.

"I've already called," Catherine said.

"Did you?"

"She did," came a voice at the officer's back.

"Francois," Catherine said.

"Catherine. Gil." Francois Beaumer shook his head and sighed. "Any idea who this is?" He shined a flashlight on the figure.

"De la Rosa," Catherine and Gil chorused.

Beaumer's eyebrows rose. "Bonus round: what's he doing dead in this car?"

"It's my car," Catherine said.

"It's her car," Gil seconded.

"I assume you don't normally transport corpses," Beaumer said to Catherine. "Don't answer that. That was poorly timed cop humor."

"How did he die, can you tell us that?" Catherine asked. "So we can get our stories straight. Don't answer that; poorly timed suspect humor."

"I'm reluctant to move the body before the techs get here. The positioning could be relevant." Beaumer stretched forward and peered into the trunk then straightened. "Could be anything but one thing appears likely: he did NikNak recently."

"I'm not surprised," Gil said. He hung his head, suddenly fatigued. His body felt leaden. Now they would never know the truth behind Ashley Slick's death and if it was proven De la Rosa was responsible for harming Alyssa, she would never see him justly punished.

"You want to tell me why, Mr. Leduc?"

"Rumors. Just rumors."

"You call them rumors. We call them leads. I will want to hear more about these rumors. But the techs are here. If you could please stand over there and give them room to work. I will want to speak with you more shortly."

The officer had Catherine and Gil positioned out of earshot so Gil couldn't hear any of the early findings.

"Assuming you didn't come back from your night out with a body in your car—" Gil started.

"I think I would have noticed," Catherine replied

"What time did you get back? I'm sure Beaumer will ask and he'll want to know where you were this evening."

"Are you interrogating me, Gil?"

"You said we should get our stories straight."

"So where were you?" You had it in for De la Rosa."

"I didn't have it in for him. I wanted to question him. And now I can't. Anyhow, I was with Jan all day, and she and Liz and I had dinner. We all called it a night because we were worn out."

"But you found him. You called me, you called the cops. What were you doing out here in the middle of the night?"

"Now who's interrogating whom?" Gil asked.

"Did you plan to go joyriding in my car?"

"Why would you suggest something like that?"

"You didn't answer my question."

"You didn't answer mine!"

"Children, children. What seems to be the problem?" Beaumer asked.

Gil and Catherine swiveled to face him.

"Ms. Robert, you may go. I'll have questions for you later; I'll be in touch. Gil, let's go inside."

Catherine mimed using her mobile phone and mouthed "Call me."

Gil and Beaumer took seats in the lobby. Behind them, the front desk phone rang constantly. Gil overheard the night clerk deliver the same information repeatedly. "Yes, sir. Yes, madame. Those lights are from police vehicles. There was an incident behind the hotel. No, sir. No, madame. Nothing to be alarmed about. You're in no danger. The police have it under control. Go back to sleep. We apologize for the disturbance."

Beaumer asked the expected questions and was particularly interested in why Gil happened to be in the parking lot at that hour.

"I couldn't sleep. I went for a walk," Gil replied, wishing it didn't sound so lame.

"In the parking lot?"

"I was going down Alles des Rochers. I spotted Catherine's car. I thought I saw the trunk ajar." That was partly the truth of the matter and it seemed to satisfy Beaumer.

The investigator pressed for details of Gil's relationship with De la Rosa.

"There was no 'relationship,'" Gil protested. "I was acquainted with him back in the States. I discovered he was now tutoring students at the institute, an interesting coincidence—"

"I don't like coincidences," Beaumer said.

"But that's all it was. I didn't study with him then or now. Are you saying I came to Royan to join him?"

"Did you?"

"He was just a face and a name. I didn't give his being here a second thought until Ashley died and I learned that De la Rosa may have been the last person to see her alive. Ashley, dead of a heart attack brought on by cocaine, you said. And Alyssa in the hospital, same thing. Is De la Rosa the connection?"

"You're asking a lot of questions and I'm looking for answers."

"So am I. Jacob said he saw Alyssa talking to De la Rosa at the Monte Carlo. Other students say De la

Rosa is the man to go to for drugs. Is he a user as well as a dealer? You said he recently used that drug, that NikNak. Did he die of a heart attack too?"

"I told you, we don't have a definite cause of death yet. I'm just going on what I saw. I can say that however the drugs got into him, it didn't happen at the scene. He was deposited there after death. We found no signs of a struggle but we did find quite a bit of scuffing on the asphalt around Catherine's car from getting the body into the car. Which was broken into, something she wouldn't need to do if she had a key."

"You can tell that?"

"Scratches and dents on the liftgate and the frame. Someone loaded him in, either after he was dead or was at least unresponsive."

"From the NikNak or was he killed some other way?"

"We have yet to find other signs of violence. It could have been an overdose and it could have been self-administered. We're calling it suspicious for now but we haven't settled on murder. We haven't precisely pinpointed the time of death either but it appears you have an alibi for the window we're working with."

"I do. I was with friends all day and evening. Jan, my girlfriend. She was with me when I found Ashley Slick. And Liz, the friend Jan traveled with."

"So you said. We'll get confirmation of course. In the meantime, you remain a person of interest."

"But not a suspect."

"Not for now. We do want you to remain available."

"What about Catherine? Why would someone dump De la Rosa's body in her car?"

"To get her in trouble with the police. Tie her up in the investigation. I imagine they hoped she'd at least be taken into custody."

"But why? Who would want to do that? Who wants her to be sidelined?" Gil glared. "Pierre. Pierre Desjardins, is that who?"

"We have had conversations with Mr. Desjardins."

"You said that but I don't see you taking any action."

Beaumer's lips thinned.

"Is Catherine a suspect?"

"A person of interest. Like yourself."

"A dead body turns up in her car and that's all she is? A person of interest?"

"Do you believe we should suspect her of being involved?"

"No, of course not! Like me, she has an alibi. She was out with … friends." At least, that was what she had told him. "You can check."

"We've been aware of Ms. Robert's whereabouts."

"You have? Have you been tailing her?"

"Tailing her? No, we don't have to. She—" Beaumer looked puzzled. "You don't know, do you?"

"Know what?" A sense of impending doom squeezed Gil's head like a vise.

Beaumer stood. "Thanks for your cooperation. That's all for now."

The detective exited the lobby. Gil was tempted to follow him to see what he could learn from the crime scene technicians but drifted back to his room instead. He stretched out on the bed but sleep was out of the question. He reached for his phone. "Was this too late to call?"

"No, I'm still up," Catherine replied. "I told you to call me. I figured you'd want to talk. How did you get on with Beaumer?"

"I didn't get arrested."

Catherine chuckled. "I gathered that."

"Neither did you." Gil paused. "Catherine, what are you not telling me?"

The other line went silent and for a moment Gil thought Catherine had hung up. At last, she said, "Not over the phone, Little Cousin. Shall we walk? It's what you were trying to do before your night went pear-shaped."

Gil agreed to meet Catherine in the lobby. The event's stress showed in her face, bare of makeup, and her hair, haphazardly pulled into a ponytail. As they left the hotel, a tow truck passed them, its lights flashing and Catherine's Peugeot on the hoist.

"That's your car," Gil said. "Is it damaged?"

"The liftgate certainly is," she replied. "But the police are taking it and impounding it. It's evidence.

"Of course."

Catherine sighed. "Once the business day starts, Job Number One will be getting a rental."

They struck off on the path between the hotel and the water, grassy fields to one side, and the rocky cliffs to the other.

"So they're taking your car into custody but not you. Is Beaumer going easy on you because you have a relationship? You and he seem well-acquainted. Did you date him too?"

Catherine gasped. "Beaumer? Gil!"

"Or was it more like Pierre Desjardins? 'Just drinks,' you said."

"Gil, why are you …? Nothing like that." She paused then took a breath and set her shoulders. "After Francois and I met on the beach that day when he asked for my identification, I followed up. I contacted him to let him know who I am."

"You're a famous actress. He knew that."

"And … something more. I want to tell you. Gil, I want to put your mind at ease and I desperately need you to be on my side in this. Before I tell you anything else, you must promise not to speak of this to a single soul."

Gil hesitated. What secret could have that had to be kept even from him? He wasn't certain he wanted to know. But Catherine's expression was pleading. "OK," he said.

"Not even Jan."

"I prom ... wait." Gil reeled back. "Not even Jan? How can I not tell her?"

"Then you'll just have to trust me without asking for further details."

Gils' head swam. Keep a secret from Jan, Jan who had been his girlfriend for years? Who had his back during previous dangerous investigations?

But now Catherine stood before him, the strain of her secret furrowing her brow and pinching her lips. "Please, Gil. Someday perhaps I can explain it to her, too. For now, though, this has to stay between us. I shouldn't even be letting you know but it's getting too awkward trying to keep you at a distance."

His girlfriend or his cousin? Which should win out, his heart or his blood? If Jan found out that he held back something important from her would she forgive him? Or would it be the end of their relationship?

CHAPTER THIRTEEN

They passed a structure that drew Gil's attention not because it was glamorous like the Belle Époque villas he showed Jan but because it stood isolated from other buildings. A humble stone construction overlooking the estuary, it was one of several crumbling World War II bunkers still dotting the Bay of Biscay coast. The fortifications had served as defenses against oncoming Allied forces during the battle and now represented something of a controversy. For some locals, they were embarrassing reminders of French harbors' humiliating roles as "Atlantic pockets" for the occupying German forces and should be torn down, removed from view, especially that of tourists. Others felt they should be preserved for their historic significance. Gil thought it appropriate to be coming upon it now. He too felt torn by conflicting emotions.

As if reading his mind, Catherine said, "You'll just have to trust her and her love for you. And you, hers. She will have to believe that as much as you hated it, it was a choice you had to make."

Every muscle in his body cramped with the strain of his dilemma. "OK, I promise."

Catherine hugged him then stepped back. "I'm a confidential informant."

"A what?" Gil gaped. "You're making this up. This is research you did for your part. Like going to driving school so you can do a better job of acting in car-chase scenes."

Catherine shook her head. "No, Gil, this is for real. This began in Tours. I assist a detective there, giving him bits of information that come to me, or looking into things, asking questions of people to whom I have access."

"Like Pierre Desjardins."

"Exactly. The Tours police believed him involved in the drug trade but he kept himself very well insulated. By getting to know him socially I was able to track his contacts and movements without him suspecting. Then he vanished from the scene. I had an inkling that he had plans for somewhere south. I guessed Marseilles but I didn't know for certain. When you said you were coming for a vacation—"

"You decided to move your operations here too? It never was about spending time with me."

"No, Little Cousin, it was. That doesn't mean I didn't keep my eyes open. When Pierre showed up, I went on high alert."

"And you sprang into action."

"Something like that. I got in touch with Francois and told him about my role in Tours. It's more than just Pierre, Gil. The two German women—"

"So you do know them?"

"Let's say they're not entirely strangers. Yes, I recognized Greta and Annalise. I have seen them on Lufthansa flights."

"They really are flight attendants?"

"They are. They're also smugglers. Geneva is a hub for cocaine trafficking."

They branched off and continued along the path, white against the dark grassy verge. Few people strolled the strand at that hour. Devoid of streetlights, the area was illuminated only by the moon and light from distant buildings. The rocks cast shadows across the sand making late-night beach-walking treacherous.

"I imagine as flight attendants it would be easier for them to sneak stuff in," Gil said.

"Not as easy as you would think. Airline personnel must go through security checks, too. They do however have insider knowledge and connections. I suspected the two women collaborate with gate agents and baggage handlers to secrete cocaine in carryons after they've been through Security but before they go on the plane, then collect the drug before the luggage is returned to the passengers. The cops are looking into that."

"Maybe Greta and Annalise got wind they were under scrutiny and that's why they checked out early."

Catherine grimaced. "Fled, you mean. I'd rather see them arrested. They'll only choose some other city as their base. But my first clue that the operation has been moved to Royan came even sooner when you mentioned the older woman on the train."

"Madame Cartier?"

"That's the one."

"She's part of it?"

"She was in Tours. Then she simply vanished. We knew she didn't die or go out of business. We were certain she set up shop somewhere else. So now, Pierre, the German women, Valerie Cartier, all in Royan. It's too much of a coincidence."

"I knew Madame Cartier was up to something." Gil felt a moment of triumph that quickly fizzled. "What exactly is she up to?"

"We suspect she is manufacturing NikNak. The fentanyl that makes it so powerful is brought in from the west, from South America and the Caribbean then combined with the cocaine."

The path dead-ended and they doubled back toward the hotel.

"She has what? A lab?"

"Probably in the villa you stumbled on. It doesn't take up much room. It does however require hazardous chemicals. We suspect she lures young men there using her lovely, lonely 'granddaughter' as bait. She gets them addicted to NikNak and presses them into service to pay for the drug. You dodged a bullet when you told her you had a girlfriend and weren't interested in meeting her granddaughter."

"But it explains why she hangs out in the institute's student lounge. Lots of solitary single young men there."

"Young men who are away from family and might not be missed if they become incommunicado."

"Right." Gil thought of the student he had noticed in the lounge and then again with De la Rosa at Madame Cartier's house. He described what he'd seen. Catherine said she would share the information with Francois.

"And De la Rosa? Was he part of the operation in Tours?" Gil asked.

"He may have been. He wasn't on my radar. Different circles, you understand. But I must have heard his name bandied about. When I saw it on the list of available tutors at the institute it rang a bell."

"Is he a dealer or a user?"

"Probably both. Most dealers are users; that's how they get into dealing in the first place. They have to support their habit somehow. It gets expensive. I don't imagine he makes much money as a tutor but he certainly is in a position to move product."

"What's your guess? Did he die of an accidental overdose or was it—?"

"Murder?" Catherine stroked her chin. "My guess? That is all it is right now, a guess. Yes, he was murdered. He was getting careless. One suspicious drug-related death and a similar crisis a day later. Two American women who have no connection save for the fact that they were both at the Monte Carlo where it's believed they both had contact with De la Rosa. It's attracted a lot of attention to the club and De la Rosa's cohorts wouldn't want that."

"The two girls had something else in common, Catherine: Jacob. He was acquainted with both of them. He and Hope were."

Catherine's forehead creased. "So were you. You and your friends are all at risk. That's what I've been trying to tell you and why I didn't want you to go to the club."

Up ahead, rickety catwalks branched out over the rocks leading to carrelets. Nets hung out from the small fishing shacks, suspended over the water, ready to be winched down at high tide.

"If it's so dangerous, why are you doing it?"

"You're not the only one who wants to follow in the footsteps of our uncle Claude and grandfather Sebastien. Working on a crime show gives me some satisfaction. We tell a story—a crime has been committed, the good guys ferret out the villain. The mystery is solved, the crooks get punished, the victims get justice, and all's right with the world again. But it's fiction, and when it happens for real right in front of you …" Catherine paused. "When that little actress died, it was tragic. So young, so full of enthusiasm and promise. One day she was raring to go and the next day she was gone." Catherine made a fist then flung out her fingers. "And for what reason? So some scumbag could line his lousy pockets, feed his ugly habits?

"I was so angry I went straight to the police to ask what I could do. I assumed they had some educational program to discourage drug use for which I could volunteer to promote, put my celebrity status to good use. 'Confidential informant' was their idea but I agreed immediately. They tell me I've been helpful, I've steered them in worthwhile directions, saved them time chasing worthless leads.

"I didn't plan to work while here in Royan. I meant to enjoy vacation time with you. But you mentioned Valerie Cartier. The German women made an appearance and Pierre showed up. I put it all together and had a visit with Francois."

"And all those times that you were scarce, you weren't in meetings or phone conferences. You were—"

"Running around Royan, keeping an eye on the bad guys. The cops, Francois, they can't be everywhere, you know that. They can't take action until they catch someone red-handed. The night I dropped you and your friends off at the club, I never did go back to the hotel. I stayed in the parking lot. I saw a truck pull up to the delivery bay."

"Desjardins said it was a shipment of sugar."

She scoffed. "Sugar, indeed. I don't doubt some of that cargo was cocaine."

Gil steeled himself to ask the next question. "Were you in the marina this morning?"

"I was. Pierre has a boat moored there. It's called High Tide."

Not the one I noticed, Gil thought, recalling his stroll through the marina with Jan.

"I don't doubt he takes it down to Spain and transports coke back in it."

"He can do that without going through Customs?"

"If they make the transfer offshore, ship to ship, out in open water. There's a lot of trafficking in Bilbao. Spain has one of the highest rates of cocaine consumption in Europe. Why do you ask?"

"Jan and I cut through the marina on our way back to the hotel. She—we thought we saw your car."

"I've been keeping tabs on when he takes the boat out and I let Francois know."

They had circled back to the hotel and stood outside the entrance. Catherine took both Gil's hands in hers. "Now you know. It's a lot to take in. And a lot to keep from Jan. But you see why you must and why you and your friends should keep your distance. For your safety and for theirs."

His head and heart in turmoil, Gil nodded. "But what about you?"

Catherine winked. "Don't you worry. I've put Francois on speed dial."

CHAPTER FOURTEEN

The friends barely made it to breakfast before the buffet was cleared. Catherine and Gil filled in Liz and Jan about the body in the car. Unlike some other hotel guests, Liz and Jan had managed to sleep through the commotion.

Liz was aghast. "How gross, Catherine. A corpse in your car." She shuddered.

"At least it was discovered before I got in it," she replied.

"And you found it, Gil. What a gruesome surprise. You have had some week. First, you come upon Ashley's body, now Mr. De la Rosa's."

"Better Gil than someone else," Jan said, munching a pain aux raisins. "Gil at least keeps his head."

Except for the few minutes I considered hiding the body, Gil thought.

"Now more than ever we're going to need Alyssa's account of what happened," Liz said. "I checked with the hospital this morning. She is being permitted visitors."

"The local car rental will deliver a ride to me," Catherine said. "As soon as it gets here, I'll give everyone a lift to the hospital."

Celeste approached the table to announce that the buffet would be closing shortly and that Catherine's car had arrived.

Catherine wiped the crumbs from her lips. "Excuse me, I'll go take care of that. Meet me outside when you're ready to leave."

The others finished their meals and exited the hotel to find Catherine lounging alongside a low-slung rose-gold vehicle.

"What is this gorgeous thing?" Liz stroked the smooth fender.

"It's a BMWi8," Catherine replied.

"They didn't have an ordinary sedan available?" Gil asked.

Catherine grinned. "I have no idea how long the cops will keep my car or if I'm even going to want to get in it when they're done. I decided to pamper myself. Besides, my insurance will pay for some of it and the rental agency said they'd cut me a deal if I would pose for some publicity shots later."

The four slid into the sleek interior.

"Wow," said Liz. "I think I could live in this. I wish the hospital were much farther away."

Catherine parked the car the furthest from the visitor entrance and took up two spaces. "I know, it's rude, it inconveniences others but the car is less likely to get door dings this way."

On Alyssa's floor, the nurse told them, "We'd prefer only two at a time. She's still getting her strength back and we don't want to wear her out."

Though he itched with impatience to ask Alyssa what she knew of De la Rosa, Gil told Jan and Liz "You two go on ahead."

"And for just a few minutes," the nurse cautioned. "We have more tests and treatments to administer. Also, the police want to talk to her."

"We'll keep it short," Liz promised.

"You can get a coffee from the vending machine at the end of the corridor," the nurse told Gil.

"Thank you," he replied but caffeine would only aggravate his tension. He settled for pacing the hallway and reading posters about early warning signs of cancers and cardiac problems.

Liz and Jan finally emerged from the hospital room. "Your turn," Jan said.

"We'll trade notes later," Liz added.

"Would you call Jacob or Hope and let them know how she's doing?" Gil asked.

"Good idea."

Gil found Alyssa looking wan, her brightly-colored hair a stark contrast to her gray complexion and dull eyes.

"Oh, honey, I'm so sorry," Catherine said. "How awful for your studies to get interrupted this way."

Alyssa gave her a weak smile. "Thanks."

"You're going to be all right?" Catherine asked. "No residual damage?"

As eager as Gil was to get answers to his burning questions, he had to give Catherine credit for being solicitous.

"A little," Alyssa replied, her voice feeble. "It will take time to heal and some effort on my part. But I should be OK."

"I'll get right to the point," Gil said. "Did De la Rosa give you the cocaine?"

Alyssa nodded. "So stupid of me. You know how sometimes when you're away from home or on vacation it's like normal rules don't apply. I don't know what I was thinking. I wasn't thinking. But he said he was a teacher. He said he knew you, Gil. I figured it would be OK."

Gil scowled. "He didn't know me, not really.

"Don't blame yourself, dear," Catherine said. "You're not the only one who fell for his sales pitch. Anyway, he won't be hurting anyone else like that again." She related the events of last night.

Alyssa blanched. "Like, I hope they don't think I had anything to do with that."

Catherine patted the sheet over her knee. "No one's suggesting anything of the sort. It's a possibility he died of an accidental overdose. Too much of his own medicine."

"That's terrible," Alyssa said. Gil was glad she didn't ask how a dying De la Rosa ended up in Catherine's car.

The four drifted back to the parking lot, sobered by the dramatic damage the drug had caused their friend and the news about De la Rosa.

"Where to next? Back to the hotel?" Catherine asked.

"I need to get a cab and get to the train station," Liz said.

Gil and Jan gaped.

"The train? Where are you going?"

"Paris. Alyssa's parents are flying in. I told them I'd meet them and travel back to Royan with them."

Catherine dismissed that with a wave. "No cab, no train. I'll drive you. I can get you to Paris in a third of the time and bring you all back."

"But they don't arrive until early tomorrow. That means an overnight stay."

Catherine tapped her chin and gazed skyward. "Hmm. Let me think about that. Two gals on their own for the night in Paris. Whatever would we do with ourselves?"

Liz threw her arms around the woman. "Oh, Catherine, that would be astounding. Thank you."

"We'll head back to the hotel, throw together some overnight things, and get going."

Liz punched the air. "Road trip!"

Catherine turned to Gil. "What about you two?"

He checked the time on his phone. "Actually, could you drop Jan and me at the marina?"

Jan narrowed her eyes. "What have you got up your sleeve, Buddy?" she asked.

"It's a surprise but I think you'll like it."

###

Gil and Jan strolled through the marina. Gil scanned the parking lot for a red Citroen and was relieved not to see one.

"It's a lovely day for a walk," Jan said, "and it brightens my mood to be in the sun and fresh air after being in the hospital but do you have a destination in mind?"

"I do," Gil said.

"And that would be?"

"You'll see." They had a few minutes to spare and Gil had to satisfy his curiosity as they ambled down and back several docks. Finally, Gil spotted what he had been looking for: Pierre Desjardin's boat. Not the biggest vessel in the marina but not the smallest either. Even with his limited knowledge of boats, Gil was prepared to say Desjardin's was deluxe, being trimmed with polished wood and boasting a cabin. The striping on the vessel's side made it look like it could race through the water. Gil imagined the two motors suspended from the stern lent more practical assistance when speeding away from covert drug buys.

No one was on deck. Gil wondered if the boat was unoccupied. He would have liked to slip aboard and snoop. Then he spotted two opened beer bottles on the deck and decided occupants could be below.

He strode up to the kiosk for La Reine de les Croisières and presented his ticket.

"Great," said the clerk. "You're the last two so now the skipper can get underway."

"Up for a boat ride?" Gil asked Jan.

"Sounds delightful. Are we just cruising the estuary?"

"Nope. We're headed there." Gil pointed out over the water.

Jan's hand flew to her mouth. "The lighthouse?"

"Yup. You seemed interested in a tour."

Jan threw her arms around him. "Buddy! When did you have time to arrange this?"

"That little detour I made before we went on the Gran Roue."

Jan's eyes twinkled. "You sly dog, you! I'm so excited. Let's go."

The two boarded the Queen of Cruises and joined the other tourists who chose seats atop the passenger cabin. The public address system crackled.

"Welcome aboard La Reine de les Croisières. I'm your skipper, Guillaume. Just a few words before we depart." He pointed out the safety features of the vessel and the location of life vests. "We anticipate a fairly smooth voyage. We'll bring the boat as close as possible and a launch will take you to the causeway but you will have to walk the rest of the way. You were notified: the jetty to the island on which the lighthouse rests can be wet and muddy so we hope you took the advice seriously and are wearing boat or athletic shoes."

Jan stuck out her legs and waggled her sneakered feet. "With all the walking we've been doing I've worn nothing but."

Summer Danger

"Changing tides mean it is of paramount importance that you be at the embarkation point at the appointed time. Any later and you will lose your window for departure. If you're late we will go on without you and you will miss the boat." Skipper Guillaume cackled.

"I wonder how many times a week he cracks that joke," Gil said.

"It will take us about forty-five minutes to arrive so relax and enjoy the ride."

Two of the other passengers had packed for a full day. The man opened a cooler and handed his companion a slim can. "Sparkling wine," he said to Gil with a grin. "Not Champagne, exactly, of course, but close enough."

"Champagne in a can. What will they think of next?" Jan asked.

"Care for one?"

"That's so kind but we're … we don't drink alcohol," Gil replied.

"I've got sodas, too. We're happy to share if you want some."

The man's companion held out a plastic-wrapped plate. "Help yourself," she said. "I call them Ship Shape Cookies."

And they were, triangular and iced to look like sailboats.

"Do you make this trip often?" Jan asked.

"It's one of our favorite ways to spend a day," the woman replied.

Jan leaned back, munched her cookie, and sipped her soda. "Oh, Gil, this is heaven."

Gil ached to share what Catherine had told him. He felt the strain in the tight muscles of his shoulders and back. He filled his lungs with salty air and let the sun melt away his tensions. The sea breeze was brisk and he would have described the crossing as "choppy" rather than "fairly smooth," lending credence to the estuary's reputation as subject to strong currents, making navigation a challenge.

The lighthouse came into view. Several privately-owned vessels were already anchored within range. Skipper Guillaume made another announcement. "You're nearly there. Thank you, people, for choosing the Queen of Cruises. Again, be careful on the jetty. It can be slippery. If you feel more secure barefoot, do not hesitate to remove your shoes. You can put them back on when you arrive at the lighthouse. There is no need to hurry. You have plenty of time to connect with the tour guide. Again, be at the departure point promptly at the conclusion. Meanwhile, enjoy your visit."

Gil, Jan, and the other passengers rode the small launch and disembarked onto a causeway. They picked their way across a wet gritty surface pockmarked by puddles. As they neared their goal, seawater splashed up onto the path deep enough to circle their ankles and Gil could imagine that when the tide came in, the jetty would be well underwater. The path led to a slit in the circular stone base on which the lighthouse perched and then to an equally narrow entrance between two stone columns.

They joined other tourists grouped around the guide.

"Welcome to Le Phare. Please stay with me," the guide said. "Do not wander off on your own and please don't touch anything. As you can imagine, some of the surfaces and structures are fragile. Le Phare has stood the test of time. You don't want to be the one who damaged what the years and tides have not."

As protection against visitors who didn't take the caution seriously, some areas were barricaded by thick ropes suspended between brass stanchions.

"This first floor is called the reception salon. We will visit all the different levels: the Girondins hall; the royal chapel and its fabulous stained-glass windows; the royal apartment, not to mention the breathtaking vista once you get to the top. From there, you'll be able to enjoy an impressive view over land and sea, one of the most spectacular in the region."

The guide set forth and the tourists dutifully followed, oohing and ahhing. They branched off to the right and Gil thought he saw a figure appear in the entrance then dart to the left. When no one joined them he decided it must have been a trick of light and shadow.

CHAPTER FIFTEEN

They passed through a door which led to a hallway.

The guide said, "Those stairs will take us up to the lantern level. There are 301 steps to the top. Don't be intimidated by the thought of all that climbing. There are several landings where you can pause if need be and we will take our time to enjoy each level."

"Unlike the stairs in the Covent Garden tube station in London," Jan murmured. "Once you start up, there's no stopping until you get to the top. Was that ever a climb!"

The guide continued. "Four small rooms on this floor were once used by the keepers. Today's keepers have a base camp near the top of the lighthouse. They now work in pairs, two weeks on and one week off during the season. They greet visitors like you, do routine maintenance, are on watch day and night to prevent vandalism and theft, and, of course, tend to the light. They're members of the Syndicat Mixte pour le Développement Durable de l'Estuaire de la Gironde. Often they give the tour but today you have me, a SMIDDEST volunteer.

"Note on both sides of the room the fountains in the form of lions' heads and made of bronze. All the rainwater which lands on the lighthouse is returned into these fountains and then stored beneath your feet. This fresh water is vital for the lighthouse keepers. I'd also like to call your attention to the sculpture over the door."

A beautiful woman's head finely carved in the stone crowned the entrance. Everywhere Gil looked he saw embellishment and adornment. Even the floors were exquisitely tiled. He was astounded that someone had gone to so much trouble to beautify what was essentially a workplace, a practical structure, adding ornamentation that would be seen by few other than the keepers. Luxury constructions in the US aimed to astound onlookers with size and ostentatiousness whereas here, even the most commonplace object was crafted to delight the viewer. It was one of the things he loved about France.

As if reading his mind, the guide said, "This is called the King's Apartment. The planner had the idea of the lighthouse serving as a royal place of residence. However, no king ever stayed here."

Stained glass windows depicting Saints Anne, Michael, Sophia, and Peter and a painted vaulted ceiling decorated the chapel. Gil would have liked to stay in the chapel and put it to its intended use, sending up prayers for Ashley and Alyssa, but the guide didn't linger.

"Next, we're headed for the third floor, the Girondin Room. The construction of this level added to the lighthouse's total height making it more visible to navigators. Here you'll want to note the heart-shape of the stair-vault which you can see if you look up."

Every head tipped backward.

"The counterweight room housed the mechanism that powered rotating screens. They created the flashing effect. The keepers had to rewind the counterweight every three hours."

The guide continued to climb the staircase. "Now this room served to store the lamp equipment. And in this room, the keepers kept an eye on the lantern to ensure it remained lit. They used a mirror system so they could check on it without having to leave the room."

The wood paneling and floor lent the keepers' quarters a warm, cozy feeling. A dining area with a dining table and four chairs flanked by rich wooden sideboards was roped off.

"And here we near the lantern itself. Once it was fueled by burning oak chips in a metal container then by a mixture of whale, olive, and rapeseed oil, and after that by petroleum gas. You will be glad to know the keepers did not have to carry the fuel up all those stairs. It was hoisted up by a pulley system through the circular openings around which the stairs wrap. Now it is fully electric. You might be surprised to learn that the light is a 250-watt halogen bulb. You might think that's not bright enough but thanks to the Fresnel lens it can be seen from as far away as 40 kilometers. It's very delicate and expensive so the lantern room is not open to the public. You can however go out on the gallery. From there you can gaze across the estuary of the Gironde and points all along the coast from the forest of La Coubre to Le Verdon-sur-Mer. The waters can be treacherous so you can imagine how welcoming the sight of the lantern was to sailors."

The tourists threaded out to the platform, jostling to exchange positions and views. Anchored to a sand island at the north end, Gil spotted a vessel he hadn't seen on their arrival. "That's Pierre Desjardin's boat," he said. Even at this distance, the racing stripes along the side were recognizable.

"And you know that how?" Jan asked.

Gil was about to reply when the guide announced "Let's head back down. The tide will be coming in which will submerge the jetty. Those of you who took the Queen over will want to be at your embarkation point to catch the launch. Don't worry, we'll get you there in plenty of time. We don't have to rush. You can revisit any of the features that caught your attention our first time through and please feel free to ask any questions that have arisen."

Gil wanted to tell Jan but he didn't want to reveal Catherine's secret with so many people around to hear. He hooked her arm and let the tourists drift down the stairs to the lower levels then motioned for her to follow.

As they descended the stairs, Gil told Jan about Catherine's undercover role.

Jan came to a standstill and gaped. "And here I thought she was up to no good and you were turning a blind eye. Instead, she's putting her time and energy into helping the police. That explains why neither she nor you were arrested in connection with the death of De la Rosa, even though his body was found in her car and you were the one who found it. I am so sorry if I spoke unkindly. Gil, I should have trusted you."

Gil breathed a sigh of relief that Jan wasn't angry. "Please, don't apologize. I should have trusted you and told you as soon as I found out but Catherine swore me to secrecy. She didn't want to put you at risk. But how could I keep it from you? It was torturing me. And given everything that's happened, she needs all the allies she can get."

Jan's brow furrowed. "If Desjardins' boat is here, where is he?"

"Good question. When we started the tour I thought I glimpsed someone coming into the reception salon. I told myself it was my imagination working overtime until I saw his boat. Now I know that must have been him but I haven't seen him."

"He must be somewhere. We should alert the keepers."

"You go. I'll scout around to see if I can spot him."

Jan wagged her index finger. "Scout only. Do not approach! No confrontations, OK, Buddy? Text me the minute you locate him. Promise?"

"I promise," he replied, and it was a promise he planned to keep. Desjardins represented more danger than Gil wanted to entangle Jan in.

Jan charged up the stairs toward the watch room. Gil hurried down to the Gironde Room. The black and grey marble floor was bare and the room unfurnished.

The only place to hide was under the staircase and no one huddled there. Gil moved on to the chapel.

Its marble floor was even grander than the Gironde room. Tables bearing simple candle holders with white wax tapers were tucked into niches. More candles lit the alcove in which a statue of Mary with the baby Jesus presided over an altar festooned with flowers. A lectern stood nearby and ladder-backed chairs with rush seats lined the walls. In the peaceful room, crafted with palpable reverence and lit softly by candles and sun filtered by colored glass, it was hard not to be humbled. Gil felt his pulse slow as he approached the altar.

"Yes, you should say your dying prayers now," came a voice at his back. Gil wheeled around to face the speaker and knew he had been right the first time he suspected that a latecomer had arrived at the lighthouse. But he was wrong about who it was.

The man holding a gun was George Arnaud.

His pulse rocketing, Gil struggled to get his brain back in gear. "You're not going to fire that around here?" he said. "A stray bullet could ruin priceless artifacts."

"That's what you're worried about?" Arnaud said.

The possibility that anything in the chapel could be damaged alarmed Gil but more importantly, he needed to stall Arnaud while he figured out how to escape. Somehow he had to distract Arnaud so he could get his phone out and text a warning to Jan.

"Don't worry. For one thing, I won't miss. But we'll take care of business elsewhere. Leaving a corpse here would only bring the law down on the lighthouse. I don't need that. Not as effective as leaving a body in Catherine's car."

"You killed De la Rosa?"

"He became a liability. The man couldn't follow the program. His job was to get customers, not kill them. He attracted too much attention. Had to go. So do you. You keep nosing around where you shouldn't even though everyone tells you to back off. Now get moving." Arnaud gestured with the gun.

"Where are we going?"

"To the boat."

"Is Pierre onboard or are we meeting him here?"

"Eager to see Pierre, are you?"

Gil wasn't. He was terrified that Jan would run into the man.

"Sorry to disappoint. Your meddling foiled our plan to get Catherine arrested and out of our hair. Pierre is taking care of her."

Gil released the breath he held and inhaled deeply. That was pure bluster on Arnaud's part. He had no idea Catherine was safe in Paris picking up Alyssa's parents.

"I'm the only one going for a boat ride. You're going for a swim. The next time you'll touch land is when your half-eaten bloated corpse washes ashore and who knows where that will be? Wherever the currents take you. One thing's for certain. No one there will have a clue as to your identity and they won't work very hard to figure it out. They'll assume you're some fool who snorted too much NikNak, went boating, and got in over his head." Arnaud guffawed at his joke.

They started down the stairs. The narrow width accommodated only one person on each tread. Gil went first with Arnaud at his back. He doubted Arnaud would shoot him here. That would cause an uproar and Arnaud would find his escape impeded.

Gil patted his pocket, fumbling for his phone to alert Jan.

"Oh no, you don't. No calling for the cavalry. Put your hands where I can see them," Arnaud growled.

Gil held his arms out to his side, his brain clicking away. The level below was the King's apartment. Gil tried to remember what he had seen of that and where he could find cover. He recalled elegant sculptures, carvings, and stonework but no furniture, hangings, or draperies behind which he could hide and contact Jan.

Ahead was a tight curve. For a nanosecond, he would be out of Arnaud's sight. Gil dropped to his belly and flattened himself on the stair tread. Arnaud would trip on or over him; either way, the man would lose his footing and Gil could get the upper hand.

At the same moment, he heard "Gil, get down!" Arnaud did indeed fall on him. He lost hold of his gun which clattered down the stairs. Arnaud went tumbling after. Gil popped up to his feet. Below him, Arnaud lay sprawled unmoving across several stair treads. A few steps above, Jan stood gripping a brass stanchion like a Valkyrie brandishing a sword.

Gil bounded over Arnaud and grabbed the gun. "How did you—?"

"I found the keepers. They were out cold and tied up. I figured Desjardins got to them. I knew he had to be around somewhere. I thought you might be in trouble." She shook the stanchion. "This was the only weapon I could find." She peered at the man lying at Gil's feet. "That's not Pierre. That's Arnaud, the bouncer from the club."

"More than a club bouncer, apparently. A murderer, an assassin."

"Is he ... did I—? All I did was whack him across the shoulders."

"That was some swing. Liz and Alyssa would be proud."

"Gil, he had a gun on you!"

"Yeah, but you had my back. As always."

Arnaud lay still. The gun in one hand, Gil tested for a pulse with the other. "No, he's alive. I don't know how long he'll stay unconscious. I'll keep the gun on him. You get the ropes that went with that stanchion and we'll tie him up."

They lashed Arnaud to a chair tighter than a caterpillar in a cocoon then raced back to the keepers' quarters. "Did he give them NikNak?" Gil asked as they sprinted up the stairs.

"I don't know. They were both unconscious. I couldn't do anything for them and I thought I'd make sure you weren't in trouble."

"I'm glad you did."

They found one keeper still blacked out, the other coming around. Gil and Jan removed their bonds and helped the conscious one to a chair.

"How do you feel?" Gil asked, dreading to hear the heart attack symptoms Alyssa reported.

"Dazed," the keeper reported. "A little nauseated."

His heart racing, Gil feared exposure to NikNak but didn't see the telltale pink froth around the keeper's nose. "That man—"

"Did he make you inhale a powder?" Jan asked.

He shook his head. "No. Something chemical on a cloth he pressed over my face. Vapors. Sweet, perfume-y. I guess I passed out." He shook his head.

"Could you find me some water? To wash this taste out of my mouth and throat."

Jan ran to find the keeper something to drink. Gil checked the pulse of the other keeper and found it faint but steady. The man moaned and tried to rouse himself.

"Who are you?" the first keeper asked. "What happened?"

"I'm Gil and this is Jan. We were on the tour. You were disabled by, well, I'm afraid he was after us." Gil explained who George Arnaud was and about his involvement in drug trafficking with Desjardins. "We've got him tied up in the chapel."

"Here, drink this," Jan said, holding a glass of water to the man's lips.

"Thanks, I'm feeling a little better. I'm Gaspar. How's Oscar?"

"Oh, my head hurts," Oscar groaned. "What happened?"

"If you two were on the tour, you'd better get going or you'll miss your ride back." Gaspar checked at his wristwatch. "Oops, too late."

"Never mind us, do you need emergency medical help? Whom should we call?"

"We should call the police," Jan said.

"You said this Arnaud and this other man have been transporting cocaine by boat?" Gaspar asked.

"Looks that way," Gil said. "The boat is still at anchor."

Gaspar glanced at his woozy colleague. "This is a job for the Coast Guard. Help me to my desk, I'll radio them. They can check us out, take this Arnaud into custody, and seize his boat."

"Francois isn't going to like that," Gil said.

"Francois?"

"Francois Beaumer. City detective. He'll want Arnaud for murder."

Gaspar gave him a wry smile. "Jurisdictional dispute. Not my problem. I just want the lowlife and his wretched boat off my island. And you two need a lift home. Unless—"

"Unless what?"

Gaspar's smile broadened. "You could stay here for the night and one of us can bring you back in the morning."

Jan's jaw dropped and her eyes widened. "Spend the night in a lighthouse? Oh, Gil!"

CHAPTER SIXTEEN

Gil called Catherine to bring her up to speed. "While they deplored what the keepers' were put through and the tense moment Jan and I had, the Coast Guard officers were glad to have justification to arrest Arnaud. They've had their eye on Pierre's boat for some time but never could catch him in the act. Now they have the boat and don't doubt they'll find plenty of damning evidence aboard."

"I'm happy to hear Arnaud is under wraps. What about Pierre?"

"He wasn't on the boat. He must still be in Royan. When we get back, I can search him out."

"Oh, no you don't, Gil. You had one close call too many. I'll contact Francois and fill him in."

"Where are you, anyway? I hear noise in the background."

"Nowhere in particular. Just taking in the Parisienne street scene. Liz says she's had enough of clubbing for a lifetime. Tomorrow we'll pick up Alyssa's parents and head straight back to Royan. We'll stop at the hospital first then get them checked into the hotel. What about you and Jan?"

"Oscar, one of the keepers, thinks he can get us back in time for us to get to church. And do I ever need it."

"OK. Let me know when you get back to the hotel."

###

Gil, Jan, Liz, Jacob, and Hope sat sipping celebratory drinks on the hotel's deck overlooking the pool and beyond it, the sea. The sound system played at a low volume that didn't drown out the rumble of the surf or the whisper of the wind in the trees and the soft lighting didn't compete with the moonlight and the phosphorescence of the waves.

After trans-Atlantic traveling then visiting Alyssa, her jet-lagged parents called it an early night and retired to their room, reassured that with rehabilitating therapy their daughter would recover.

Jacob lifted his champagne glass. "Here's to George Arnaud having to pay for his crimes."

"And to Jan and Gil for bringing him to his knees," Hope said.

"Literally. Knocked that one out of the park," Liz added and winked at Jan.

The others raised glasses of bubbly and nonalcoholic sparkling wine and tapped the rims together in a toast.

"That was great the keepers let you spend the night there."

"Trust me, you do not want to live in a lighthouse," Jan said.

"No?" Liz's face was creased with disbelief. "You didn't enjoy your stay?"

"Oh, we did. What a once-in-a-lifetime experience. The sounds, the smells, even the temperature. Like being in another world entirely. But those keepers? They work constantly. They're always on alert. And they have to know so much. Not just how to operate the light but all-around maintenance for keeping the lighthouse in repair. How to maintain and pilot a boat, how to navigate those waters in any kind of weather. They're custodians of the island's fragile environment. And they have to be creative and flexible because, well, if they run out of something or something breaks, they can't just jump in the car and make a Walmart run," Gil said.

Liz pressed her lips together. "Hmmm. I never thought …"

"I know," Jan said. "You were picturing long tranquil days in a window seat, staring out to sea, and writing."

Liz laughed. "You know me too well."

"Where did you go while you waited for Alyssa's parents to land? Did you visit the Louvre?" Jan asked.

Liz shook her head.

"The Eiffel Tower?"

"Nope."

"Notre Dame?"

"Uh uh."

"So where did you go? Shopping?"

"In a way." Liz's face broke into a grin. "We went to a bookstore."

"A bookstore? You were in Paris and you went to a bookstore?"

"The most fabulous bookstore ever. From the outside, it looks like just a little old bookshop but inside it's huge. New books, antiquarian books, best sellers, obscure indie titles. They've got it all. It was started—well, restarted—by an American. All the famous ex-pat writers have hung out there: Allen Ginsburg, William Burroughs, Anais Nin, James Baldwin." Liz pressed her palms together and gazed upward. "You can sleep there, in a book nook. They have benches that convert into a bed. Sweet dreams, surrounded by books! I could live there."

"I thought you wanted to live in Catherine's car."

"That too. I could have bought a million books but how would I get them home? I got a book bag instead." She reached under the table and held up a canvas bag for all to see. In blue ink, a line drawing depicted the shop's façade and the store's name: Shakespeare and Company.

Jan rolled her eyes. "Writers. You're in the City of Lights and you go to a bookstore. "

"Speaking of Catherine, where is she?" Liz asked.

With a conspiratorial look, Jan glanced at Gil.

"Probably sacked out after all that driving," he replied. At least he hoped she was. He'd been playing telephone tag with her all day. She texted him from the hospital. He replied he Oscar delivered him and Jan to Royan. At the conclusion of the church service, he found her response. He texted that he and Jan were grabbing a late lunch at a cafe on their way back to the hotel but didn't hear from her after that. "I'll send her another text. That might not disturb her if she's resting." He fired up his phone. He was about to message her when the device chimed a notification. An incoming message was from Catherine. Finally, he thought with relief and clicked on it.

His elation plummeted as he scanned the text.

"If U want 2 C Catherine again meet me on the promenade. come alone. Pierre."

Pierre had Catherine's phone? Pierre must have Catherine! Gil strained to see across the pool and spotted what appeared to be Pierre's Citroen parked along the path between the hotel and the rocky cliffs overlooking the beach, the track he and Catherine walked the night he found De la Rosa. From where Gil sat he couldn't tell if the car was occupied.

He texted back. "How do I know you have her?"

Pierre replied with an image: Catherine seated in what appeared to be a car's interior. Light filtering through the window showed her to be gagged and bound.

"Gil, what's wrong? That call looks like it's bad news," Jan said.

Gil held up his hand to hold off further questions. Stalling for time while his brain scrambled for a response Gil texted, "How do I know that's not Photoshopped?"

A notification alerted Gil to an incoming video chat from Catherine. Due to conflicting schedules and the difference in time zones, they rarely chatted live in the past but they had used it a few times. He clicked on the call. Catherine's face appeared on the screen. Her wriggling told Gil she was alive. The gag prevented her from speaking but her scowl, the fire in her eyes, and her shaking head spoke for her.

The chat ended. Pierre texted "satisfied?"

Gil replied. "I'm coming." He put away his phone and stood. "Pierre's got Catherine," he said. "He wants me to meet him."

Jan gasped. "Where?"

Gil pointed.

"I'm coming with you."

"No, no. Don't any of you follow me. If he sees anyone besides me he'll just take off with her for who knows where. But call Francois Beaumer. Tell him what's going on. He'll know how to intervene without jeopardizing the situation."

"I've got his contact number," Jacob said.

"We can see you from here. If we get any hint that you're in trouble, we're right behind you."

Fear and fury battled for Gil's will. Fury won. "Desjardins is the one who's in trouble."

His friends punched the air and hastened to the railing at the edge of the deck to get a better view of the scene.

Gil raced downstairs, through the entrance, and cut across a grassy field.

The Citroen stood partly shadowed by a copse. At Gil's approach, Pierre emerged and hauled Catherine from the vehicle. He hooked her elbow with one arm and pointed a gun at Gil with the other. "Let's go," he said.

"Where?"

Desjardins pointed with the weapon. "Go." Gil stepped forward. For the second time in two days, he had a gun at his back. He moved into the copse. Despite the balmy temperature he shivered with the conviction that Pierre planned to shoot them both and leave their bodies hidden by the trees while he escaped.

"You idiot, Catherine," Desjardins said. "You could have made this so much easier on yourself. You could be in a nice cozy cell awaiting trial for murder instead of on your way to a watery grave."

So he wasn't going to shoot them here, Gil realized.

Beyond the grove, to the right and left, stone outcroppings sloped down to a rocky shoreline. A head injury and drowning could easily be explained by someone losing his footing on the slick surface, smacking his head on a rock, and tumbling into the surf to be washed out to sea. The boulders bracketed a patch of gritty chalky sand, white in the moonlight, and just past that, a path led to a boulevard. Gil thought he could make a break for it, aim to reach the street where he might be able to stop a driver on a late-night outing, or get help from someone in the neighboring homes. But what about Catherine?

He half-turned. Catherine wasn't making Pierre's job easy. She dragged her feet and tugged at his grip.

"Don't try my patience, woman," Desjardins growled. "And you keep walking, mister. You shouldn't even be here. Arnaud was supposed to take you out of the picture."

"But he screwed up."

"Yeah, he screwed up. And got my boat impounded. Ach," he said and spit. "The man was a disaster as an enforcer. Way too busy chasing skirts."

Gil wasn't about to argue. That was what he remembered from Arnaud's tenure at the store where they both worked.

"Just goes to show. If you want something done right, do it yourself. Move."

"I'm trying," Gil said. "The rocks are slimy."

"Oof!"

Gil whirled to find Catherine on her rump. She had slipped, pulling Desjardins to his knees along with her. He struggled to his feet and tugged at Catherine.

Gil seized his chance and sprinted across the sand.

"Get back here," Desjardins hollered. He stuck his arm out and fired. A bullet smacked the ground around Gil and sent sand spraying.

"Catherine, run," Gil shouted. He glanced over his shoulder to see his cousin get to her feet and spring to the cover of the trees. Desjardins swiveled left then right as if trying to decide whom to pursue. He fired off another shot into the trees.

Summer Danger

Gil listened for a wounded cry but none came and he prayed the shot went wild. He risked another glimpse backward to see that Desjardins had chosen him as his target. Gil made tracks. Ahead a path shone white in the dim light. Gil followed it hoping it led to the boulevard. His spirits plunged when it came to an abrupt end at the rocky slope.

To his left, a grassy field was a dark open patch devoid of cover. He looked to his right. A flight of steps led to a catwalk terminating in a fishing carrelet. Maybe he could find something with which to shield himself and perhaps a weapon. Fishermen used knives … Gil bounded up the wooden steps and across the narrow rickety footbridge.

Not far behind, Desjardins fired off a third shot. The bullet struck wood with a crack. Shards stung Gil's ankle.

He reached the hut. He tugged at the wooden door and when it refused to budge, threw all his weight against it. It yielded and he stumbled into the small room, dark save for moonlight through one narrow window.

"You won't escape me there, Leduc," Desjardins hollered. "That's a dead end. You're trapped!"

Desjardins was right. The flimsy table, chairs, and narrow cot offered a place to sit and enjoy refreshments with a friend or take a nap while the net did all the work but nowhere to hide. There could be a knife somewhere but Dejardins would be on him before he could find it.

Gil flung open the small door to the sea, tripped on the splintered deck, and crashed against the wooden railing. The old weathered wood cracked. He flailed his arms to regain his balance and keep from flipping over the railing into the sea. The deck left him just enough room to stand between the hut and the railing. In front of him, hanging from a metal beam that extended over the water, the net swayed in the breeze. Behind him, the stairs creaked under Desjardins' weight.

Desjardins pounded across the catwalk. The cabin's wooden floor squeaked.

Gil darted to the right, planning to slip around to the hut to the catwalk, down the stairs, and race back to the hotel. But the railing and the deck didn't wrap completely around the hut. Barely two feet of open deck space and railing ran alongside the hut which stretched across the width of the deck. He flattened himself against the side of the hut in the few free inches of clear space.

Desjardins thrashed inside the hut. Gil heard him turning over the chairs, the table, the cot. "You can't hide, Gil!"

Where could he go? Gil craned his neck over the railing. From here he couldn't judge the depth of the water. He could scale the railing and drop into the water only to crash against rock. Crippled, he would be at Desjardins' mercy.

The hut's rear door slammed open. Gil risked a glance over his left shoulder. Desjardins stepped onto the deck. "You came out here thinking you could escape but there's nowhere to go," the man said. He stood against the broken railing and peered into the water. "Decided to take your chances with the sea? Good luck with that. Saved me the trouble."

Gil lunged behind Desjardins. With the flat of his hands and the bottom of one foot on the man's back, he shoved. The weakened timber gave way.

"Hey!" Desjardins cried as he fell through the opening and dropped into the fishing net. Something hit the water with a splash. Gil hoped it was Dejardins' gun.

Gil maneuvered the support beam to position the net over the water, out of reach of the hut.

Desjardins yelled, cursed, and wriggled against the net but his struggles only worsened his entanglement. Gil found the winch and counterweight and lowered the net so its cargo dangled partway into the water. Even if Desjardins managed to untangle himself from the net, he'd have to climb the wires from which the net hung to reach the beam then hand-over-hand his way along it to regain the deck.

Footfalls on the catwalk stopped Gil's racing heart. Who was coming? Did Desjardins have an accomplice? Could it be Madame Cartier?

He wheeled and faced Francois Beaumer.

"You're OK?" Beaumer asked.

"Yes," Gil panted.

"Catherine's OK. Shaken but unhurt. She said you took off in this direction. I heard shots. Where's Desjardins?"

Gil pointed.

Beaumer peered over the side of the broken railing. "Hmm." He turned to Gil. "Nice catch."

CHAPTER SEVENTEEN

Gil and Catherine stood a safe distance away and watched as firefighters and law enforcement personnel converged on the scene. Emergency crewmembers hustled to the site only to be shooed back, allowed to return after they donned protective gear and were briefed by supervisors. Francois Beaumer, along with other sergeants and captains wearing headsets and armed with walkie-talkies, clipboards, and tablets, shouted and pointed. Reporters clamored for access. From behind barricades, photographers and videographers got what images they could using zoom lenses.

Gil wished he had a face mask and goggles like the ones the cops and firefighters wore. Even where he stood the acrid smoke stung his nostrils and made his eyes water. "They didn't find any bodies?" Gil asked.

"Not that I'm aware of, no." Catherine gazed upward. "They haven't finished searching so I suppose they still could. If people were working in the lab …" She shuddered.

"But that young man, the one I asked you about, that I saw here with De la Rosa …?"

"Still missing as far as I know. The police will keep looking for him."

"At least he's not dead," Gil muttered. "You don't think Arnaud had something to do with this, do you?"

"I don't see how, not personally. He is in custody and he won't be seeing daylight for a long time. Ashley Slick's and De la Rosa's deaths, Alyssa's poisoning, the assaults on the lighthouse keepers, the threat against you and Jan …"

"Without whom I might not be here," Gil said.

"I owe her a debt of gratitude. That girl has guts. Speaking of keepers, she's a keeper for sure."

"Arnaud said he was 'just following orders,'"

"Orders, indeed. His habit ordered him to do whatever it took to support his addiction. As for claiming he acted on orders from Pierre, that won't buy him any clemency," Catherine replied. "Pierre's not going anywhere for a while. He's got the assaults on you and me to answer for plus a boatload of trafficking charges. Pun intended."

"And Valerie Cartier?"

Catherine growled. "Gone without a trace."

"She got away?"

"That would seem to be the case." Catherine glowered. "After all our work …" She closed her eyes then reopened them and focused on the wreckage across the street. "It's tragic. Such a lovely building."

"I'll bet the neighbors are glad their homes didn't catch fire."

"True, but their property value is going to crater and those who are leasing theirs will have a hard time finding renters."

"No one wants to live next to what was a drug lab?"

"Not only that, but the manufacturing process emits dangerous fumes that linger and continue to discharge long after the lab is shut down. I'm surprised no one noticed strange odors." She tsked. "The whole structure will have to be demolished. They'll have to call in environmental forensic technicians to see if the soil is contaminated."

"I had no idea. The gift that keeps on giving, huh?"

"This may actually have been an accident. The manufacturing process uses ether. Highly explosive if not handled with care. To control its use in drug labs like this where it's likely to be mishandled, some governments have made it available for purchase only with a license."

"Ether, huh? Do you think that's what Arnaud used to overpower the lighthouse keepers?"

"He certainly would have had access to it." Catherine hung her head. "The whole business leaves a scorched trail of damage. Users have to grapple with addiction for the rest of their lives, their bank accounts drained, their careers and families destroyed. Neighborhoods are permanently blemished. "

"I had no idea."

"I didn't either. But the more I learned about it, the more I was glad I was doing something to help."

"I am too, I guess, except ..." Gil looked at the blackened and smoking wreckage. "Catherine, it's not safe. I mean, seriously not safe. You were almost killed."

Catherine picked at her cuticle. "I know, Little Cousin. That was my bad. When you told me Arnaud and the boat had been seized, I figured I'd better keep an eye on Pierre. He got the jump on me. I learned my limits. I promise you, I won't be going anywhere near any drug dealers. I'm reconsidering my original idea of volunteering to help promote diversion and prevention programs."

Gil looked at her with narrowed eyes. "Until the next time the police ask you to play a bigger role. Like cozy up to an unapproachable club owner or get acquainted with shady flight attendants?"

"Or assist an elderly lady on a train?"

"I was just trying to be helpful."

"So was I, Gil. So was I." Catherine winked. "Who can say?"

THE END

Made in the USA
Middletown, DE
24 August 2024